MW00425064

Elaine,
I always appreciate you
catching my mistakes.
5/19/14

Nobody Says Hi Anymore:
A Viru-pocalyptic Adventure

J. Shepard Trott

Kensington Recycled Materials Co.

Nobody Says Hi Anymore

Table of Contents

1. Quik-Stop   1
2. Angie   5
3. The Best I Can Do   11
4. Hope(less) at the End of the World   17
5. Purpose   21
6. All the Times Jim Saved Me   24
7. Kwanesha, My Kung Fu Master   26
8. Fighting to the Death for Fun   29
9. Angie Again   32
10. Plan   35
11. Angie's Kindness   38
12. Warehouses vs. Apartment Buildings   41
13. Flashback   43
14. Obvious, Terrible   45
15. Zoo?   48
16. Holmesburg   52
17. Last Worker in Animal Control   55
18. Animal Traps Are Safe?   59
19. Swinging Blood Mouths   62
20. Good Trap, Bad Trap   67
21. Better Trap?   69
22. Good Cop   72
23. I'm a Mom   76
24. Forager   80
25. Maybe it was Her   87
26. Dilemma   89
27. Chasing Human (for a change)   92
28. So Many Blood-mouths   97
29. What Happened to the Baptist Army   102

30. In the Shit   108

31. Why live with guilt?   111

32. Is Angie Here?   117

33. Blow that Shit UP!   124

34. TAC TAC TAC   128

35. Up at Holmesburg   133

36. Angie?   140

37. Dusty and Me Flashback   145

38. For the Love   147

39. Eternal   150

40. Epilogue   158

1. Quik-Stop

Some people say that it started in a lab. Others say it moved from monkeys to man somehow. Like AIDS. Others say it's God's judgment. People said that about AIDS, too. The thing is, when you're running for your life, it doesn't fucking matter. It just is.

I'm standing in a convenience store. I knew this place back before, and it was shitty then, a couple dudes from India who didn't give a fuck about the people in this ghetto neighborhood, never washed anything, the stainless steel rollers in the hotdog heater had turned brown. I mean, it's stainless steel. I still ate them. They were a dollar. I shouldn't think about those hot dogs though. That shit makes me hungry real fast. Hot food doesn't happen anymore. The gas doesn't run. Smoke brings them. So I pick among the cans.

There are still so many cans, and that makes me feel two ways. One, where are the people? I mean, if no cans are being taken, then there aren't any people. That means my chance of survival is pretty low. No big fucking surprise there, but still. It'd be nice to think there was someone else out here. The other thing I think is, if no cans are being taken, there aren't any people, so at least there are lots of cans. So it's a complicated feeling.

I look for carbohydrates. I mean, I'll eat canned spinach, but you can't run real long on that. Some Chef Boy Ardee works good- a little mealy two years past its expiration date, but edible and it'll keep my energy up. I fill up my bag on that stuff, and turn my attention to the street outside.

Quiet as Hiroshima that day in 1945? 44? I wasn't that good in history. I specialized in escaping class, something that is a little more useful now. I mentioned that this used to the ghetto. The same thing that made it bad then, the many close buildings, the walls, the concrete, makes it safe living now. So many places to hide, so many fortresses to create.

The store has two sets of doors, so I go through the first one, hiding behind a smashed bubble gum machine, and a poster for a frozen fruit drink that will never be made again. The street still looks quiet, and I pop through the last door and stride, keeping low, toward an overgrown backyard. It's only a few yards of open space and I give myself an eighty percent chance of making it unseen.

I hear feet. Sprinting feet. They are coming down the main street, they haven't seen me. I could go on, but if they see me they'll know about my little duckee. Blood on the trail; their noses smell blood. It's not worth it. So I turn.

There are two of them. Now they see me. One lets out a screech. From the sound of it, she's a female, but there isn't much else to tell that. She's ripped out most of her hair. The other one is taller, and I figure he is male. The dick swinging between his legs tips me off.

They are naked. They are dirty everywhere but around their mouths, where their tongues clean a circle. The only mess around their mouths is blood, which is mostly between their teeth with small flecks like freckles on their faces. Even at a sprint, a tongue comes out periodically, licking their upper lip, leaving blood pinked saliva there. Their bodies are gashed. Their zeal in pursuit produces these cuts, as they hurdle barbed wire fences, and crash through doors with no thought to their health. Still they are whole, moving at a full out sprint. They will be on me in a moment. I almost think that they are smiling at the thought of this, but I've never seen one smile. I don't run from them much anymore. I haven't won many of those races, and then I was out of breath for what happened next.

I wish I had the sword she had in Kill Bill. Turns out most of the katana blades in North Philly bedrooms, the same rooms that are full of video games (which don't work, there is no electricity), and comic books, are worthless when it comes to actually chopping through flesh.

What I ended up deciding on, in the absence of a samurai sword that could fell seven with a single blow, is the top bar of a bike frame, with about a foot long wooden handle shoved up one end, and bolted in. The other end still has the twin bars that hold the rear wheel, but I bent them out, so that they face opposite directions. I left the bike seat bar on, and about six inches of the vertical bar of the frame. This I hammered into a spike. It's basically a spikey club, something that the first cave man would have been pretty proud of, but which I, having grown up playing Halo and shooting plasma shrapnel through the universe, knew to be corny. That was why I named it Ackee.

She lunged first, her teeth gnashing twice the in air, ready for the meal already. He was a little to my right so I stepped to the left, and swung Ackee up. It'd have been a finished blowing if not for it burying a point into one of her flailing arms. She screamed again. BITCH. DO NOT SCREAM. She's stuck to the Ackee now and he's coming at me. I rotate so that she's still between us, and Ackee is keeping me separated from her gnashing mouth. He roars in frustration. This is making too much noise.

I kick her in the chest, and she unplugs from the end of Ackee. He's at me in a second. There was a time when I made mistakes in scenes like this. When I got nervous. I didn't get better, really. A bit. The main thing that happened was, I'd been this close enough times, and I realized, "I'm going to die." After that, I was a lot calmer. I don't worry about surviving. I swing Ackee up and down into his head. Easy as you open a door. Two of the tines embed in his skull, and I pull up quick so the points twist out, breaking his skull open as he sinks down. She recovers in time to watch me send Ackee whistling into her head. THUNK. The devotion dies in her eyes.

Ackee is quiet and effective. Of course, I can't forget the screams. The pitter patter of more sprinters sounds in my ear. I decide to see if I can make the duckee. It sounds like five or six this time, and I've never faced more than three at a time.

4

2. Angie

I used to think that they were hungry, but that's not it. They're angry. Or crazy for blood. See, I was a fat guy, most of my life. It was only two months into this, the All-Fucked Era, and I'd lost a lot of weight. I was running a lot, fighting a lot, and not eating hot food, which I already mentioned. I started to look a little better, though I was sad as a dead crocodile when the Cheetos everywhere turned stale. Can you imagine, walking into a store and bags and bags of Cheetos are spilling off the shelves, and you open one up, shove a Cheeto in your mouth: Styrofoam. I still ate them.

The point is I was thinner and a little scruffy, but nobody would have called me good looking. I lived with a couple of people back then. There were more people at first. The people I lived with were older and I was sort of their kid. One guy was this fifty year old mechanic named Jim. He used these big wrenches to brain VBs. The other was Kwanesha, she was only twenty five, but she and Jim were a couple. Back then we used to joke about me being the kid, and how they had to make some babies to replenish the earth. But even then, we couldn't imagine bringing a kid into this place. Much less being pregnant. Anyway, we were at a Shoprite, getting cans, when this girl scampered down an aisle. She was really little, like four foot ten, and dirty, but clearly not a VB, because she was looking over her shoulder, not forward. VBs always look forward, at where they're going, at what they hate. The other big difference is the blood and nakedness, though you still saw some with clothes back then. They hadn't got around to shedding them.

"They're coming," she said.

"How many?" said Jim.

"I don't know."

"Estimate."

"Twenty? A lot."

"Fuck." This was the way we all felt.

"Why'd you lead them to us?" I said.

"I didn't know you were here." In her tiny hand, was a Little League Bat. The sound of crashing, of shelves being knocked over, of food stuffs flying everywhere, echoed through the store.

Kwanesha said, "Back entrance."

We followed her, with Jim taking the rear. The mini-girl got out in front. We made it into the stock room without making too much noise. I was checking out her butt as we walked along, but it was really her face that I was excited about. Maybe any female would have looked amazing to me right then. I don't know. I thought that underneath the dirt she had the most perfectly shaped lips, bright eyes. She was small, not young. I mean, she was my age- I was sixteen then.

So back to fat. Being fat sometimes is a symptom. It's funny; it being All-Fucked Era, there is a lot of time to think about your life. I don't have any social life to think about now, it's me and the not-humans. But I think I was fat because I didn't give a shit. I didn't care because I didn't think I had a chance. I didn't think I had a chance because I didn't know anything about girls. Worse, I didn't like myself. So, fat, afraid, and with no social skills I wasn't exactly going to be bagging like a ShopRite employee. Fact, girls didn't see me. Like it used to be, when you didn't see plastic bags, chip bags, blunt wrappers, on the Philly streets. They were there, but they didn't mean shit.

The girl, her name was Angie, came back with us. We lived in a row home. We stayed on the second floor, and it seemed pretty safe. For two months she thought I was really annoying, because I was. I said mean things to her all the time, like how she led the VBs to us, or like, what good would a ninety pound girl be in a fight with VBs. She mostly ignored these comments. Eventually I figured out that she didn't care what I thought, and that my technique of pretending that I believed I was better than her wasn't working.

We had a lot of time together. Jim and Kwanesha said that it was near the end and they had to get in what fun they could. They had triple boarded the back room windows, but I still worried about Kwanesha's noise. Anyway, they spent a lot of time alone together up in that room. I had some comics and old magazines but I'd read them all so many times and new reading material was something you had to risk your life for. So Angie and I were together a lot. So I decided to ask her where she was when it happened.

Angie said, "I don't want to talk about that."

I said, "We've got to do something." She was re-reading a magazine for girls and didn't respond. I added, "It's not like you're ever going to be able to get that make-up."

She looked up at me. "True," she said.

"You don't need it," I tried.

"You know that if I was Eve, and you were Adam, which is just about what it is, the human race would die?" This was no revelation to me.

"So we're stuck here with nothing to do. You might as well tell me how you survived."

She had been home alone. She had three older brothers, and her mom. Her dad wasn't home much. She was watching the news, which was talking about violent outbreaks, in prisons and hospitals. She had looked out the window, and saw the street.

She saw eight large people tear into an old couple who used to sit on their stoop. It had disturbed her and she called 911 but there was no answer. Suddenly she'd sensed that it was all coming apart at the seams, that this wasn't incidents, but everything, a pattern, and she had scampered out her back window, and up a drainpipe onto the roof. There she had huddled in a corner, and, in the warm August air, listening to screams, fell asleep.

In the morning, she could see that people wandered the streets in groups, that their eyes were vigilant, their ears attentive. They jogged and sometimes sprinted. They chased after noise, kicked in car windows. No-one was acting normal. They didn't drive. Always on foot. Vehicles were parked perpendicular to the street, or smashed into each other.

For most of us survivors, it was accidents like this. If you were in an institution, a school, at that moment, you didn't make it.

She went back in the house. One of her brothers was there. It was her favorite brother, the oldest, I forget his name, but he was the one that taught her to catch and told her to watch out for assholes but wasn't paranoid about her dating, except when she needed him to be. He would make meals for her when she was little. But it wasn't him, if you know what I mean. He looked at her and came for her. She ran back the way she came, shoving her little body back out that window, and shimmying that drain fast. When he came after her, she was ready.

This is another thing about survivors. We didn't think that long. We adapted. I'm just saying, if you spent a lot of time getting your bearings, you didn't have any. If you wept for those you lost, you died. Or you became a blood face.

She broke a brick off a chimney. She stove her brother's face in as he clambered up. The first hit, he stopped climbing. The second hit, he went down permanently.

Another thing about survivors. None of us spent too much time trying to meditate on the things that had passed away. No time for sentiment. Realism. Toughness.

9

You would think North Philly would have done better. Maybe we did. Maybe I'm the last human.

But yeah, I liked Angie. And I wasn't fat anymore. That gave me hope.

3. The Best I Can Do

I slide under the branches of a mulberry, and along into the backyard. The branches form a screen. I hear their shrieks of anger as I negotiate a hole in a wooden fence. Then I move in the back door of a house. It's actually a back opening; the door is gone. Once inside, I sprint up the stairs. They hunt with smell as well as sight. When I'm escaping, I keep moving. If they discover my scent, I've still stretched the distance between us, and I've got a chance. It's all about giving yourself a chance.

When I reach the third floor of the house, I duck through a pane-less window onto the back roof. From there I jump and pull myself up and roll onto the main roof. I allow myself a peek back. I'm now three stories above them, and one hundred feet away, and the mulberry tree is between us. There are eight of them, noses lifted into the air, peering about. They look as harmless as dogs or fat men in mental institutions, as if their gaze and sniffing are only curiosity. They haven't caught my scent. They'd be moving already. I know what will happen next. When they are alive, for some reason, they never rage against each other. Jim used to say they had the same goal of destruction, and they knew it. I heard a guy say it was pheromones. I don't know. Their eyes turn down to the two I destroyed. VBs eat anything. I've seen them chew on sneaker leather, sidewalk weeds, anything. So it's not surprising when they sink teeth into the dead. It's just something I prefer not to watch. I lower my head, and get to the middle of the roof.

I walk along the roof tops. One or two roofs are flimsy, but I know the solid beams and carefully walk them. Most of the roofs are still firm. When I get to a house with a roughly built trap door set in its roof, I swing down onto the lower roof and enter through the window. I climb down the stairs, which are littered with left-overs, picture frames with shattered glass. I see one, a group, a man, and a woman and three kids, all with the same brown hair and squinty eyes, smiling broadly. That looks bad to me. The only times I've seen anyone smile like that recently, it's 'cause they lost their brain. I enter the second floor front bedroom.

I've got it very organized. No broken shit on the floor. Weapons hang along one wall. Another is a shelf with books, and a few PSP games (one can hope). There are a few stacks of books on the floor, but they are neat and even. There is a mattress in one corner. Sheets, kind of clean. In the bureau there are a lot of different items I think I might need if I set out for somewhere. Most of the floor is clear, and swept. I wipe it down once a week. Probably, if you've got the picture of me right, you are thinking, this former fat kid who eats Styrofoam Cheetos is organized? That doesn't fit. You're right. I was that kind of kid, not just clothes and games on the floor, but food wrappers too (no wonder he struggled with finding a girlfriend). But when you live in one room, and you've read all your comics, newspapers, and books four times, you clean your room. Then you figure out, hey, this is kind of nice. And it's nice to feel like this space is in control. I don't feel like that anywhere else. I know where everything is, I know where I would put Weapon X: Issue 4, if I had it.

I hang Ackee by the door, and tip toe down the hall to the bathroom. This room reeks, 'cause I only flush once a day. I piss into the top basin. I can use the collected piss later to flush the bigger stuff. You might say, why not just throw your shit outside? They watch for that, and they've got a great sense of smell. I figure, the sewer system is still intact. That way I can live in a house, and there is no sign.

Water is easy. It rains a lot, and I've got a real clean trashcan set up so the roof drains into it. It's a bit of a risk drinking rain water off a roof, but not drinking water is a bigger risk.

I could talk a little about my defense system, but it's basically more about escape. There are trap doors in the room. One going up and another that goes down. The downward one is under a piece of plywood. I pried up some floor boards, and kicked through the plaster. It doesn't look like an escape hole from below, just your average end of the world wear and tear. The one going up is the same thing, but there it's on hinges, so I can swing it up quickly if I need to. I took the hinges off some kitchen shelves. I always use what's handy. Foraging is necessary, especially for reading, but it's also risking your life. I can exit out the windows and drop about twelve feet to the street, or out the hallway to the third or first floor. I've been here for a few months. Eventually, I'll have to leave. I could defend against a couple, but that isn't usually how it works.

The last time I had to leave a place was terrible. This was about four months back. I heard footsteps coming through the house, and I knew it was them. Weren't

13

many normals left. The visitors were coming up the stairs. Back then I lived on a third floor. I went to go onto the roof, and saw about seven of them roaming along the roofs. I ducked back down.

There were three sets of steps on the stairs. They saw me, they scream, now the team from the roofs is coming for me. First, I got real calm by thinking, "I'm going to die." After that I thought about what I was going to do.

I jumped off the half roof. It was about twenty two feet, maybe more. I landed light as I could, but I still sprained my ankle. I didn't even allow myself to whisper, "Fuck." Sprained ankle meant, they see me, I'm dead. I limped across the yard, through a hole in the fence. Then I saw they were in other houses, and on the roofs on the back of the block. It felt like I was surrounded. I did something I don't do much. It was there though. The backup plan. I went through a vacant lot, onto the street. I heard the screeches. They all started running for me. I kept hobbling, now allowing myself to curse.

On the street I hopped into a Ford 150. They were sprinting toward me. Like wolves, you know. One leapt off a roof, and landed a lot better than me, and sprinted toward the car.

Oh you fucking starter, sing for me now. Moment of terror, and the thing started. I was pulling away when one of them rammed into the window, cracking it. I swung out. Driving is hard. Lots of random vehicles in the way. I use a bigger vehicle for that reason, banging through them. I ride around the block once, slamming into the pack. After that I realized that they were hunting.

Not just roaming, hunting. They went through a block in large groups, with waiting sentries.

What they do is, get in groups of fifty or so, and they hunt a block. Some stay outside, and others run through the house. When they spot a normal person they scream, and then it's over. I've got guns, you know. But guns are a double-edged sword. You kill that one, fast and from distance, but it's just like a car. It makes a lot of noise. Each bang calls them to you. People used guns early on, but they all died, eventually. You can only have so many rounds.

Now you're saying, "Why don't you drive everywhere?" As I was smashing through them with the steel bumper on that 150, I sure liked it. The problem is, there are so many, and once they hear a car, they all come running. So once you're in a car, you got a problem. You got to stop sometime. And when you do . . . Well, that time I drove up to the far Northeast, before I ditched the car. Out there, there is a lot of space, so I could have a running start. I made it, but I don't drive much.

Beside those packs it's quiet. It's been six months since I heard VBs chase anything but cats, which means no roommates. So. Take a seat by the window, where I can see the street through the blinds. I got a Franklin busybody so I can watch the block. I have a much better exit plan if they come again. I pull out an episode of Batman. I read the dialogue blocks, and then I examine every little feature. The costumes, the positions. I try to see something I've never seen before. It's good reading. I try to ignore his softness. It always feels like he takes the death of his parents a little hard. I mean, he's still got

15

Albert. What would he do if everyone died? I sip slowly from a bottle of Coke, enjoying the sweetness and the little bit of bite left. This is home for today. It's the best I can do.

4. Hope(less) at the End of the World

Sometimes I watched Angie. Her legs looked nice. She called me a creep but I was only doing what boys have always done. I told Angie, about a week after she told me she wouldn't be with me even if I was the last man, "You shouldn't have said that."
"What?"

"That I had no chance."

"I was just trying to be real with you."

"Yeah, but now I've got nothing to live for." It was a bitch-ass thing to say, but hopeless people say those things.

"Yeah you do. Stop being a baby. You can live to kill these VBs so we can have the city back."

Jim, Kwanesha, and I first met in a group of people that followed this guy. He was a big man, some kind of Baptist preacher, with a beard that looked tough. His signature weapon was a truck jack, and he swung that thing like God's own hammer.

His people were pretty organized and they picked us all up at different points, and we all got the same speech at different times. "I'm Pastor John. I don't know what you believe, but I believe in a God that cares about us. He wants to save us, and we are about salvation. Even if you don't believe in God, you got to agree, this city is a mess; these crazies are tearing it to pieces. It wasn't meant to be this way, and we've survived, I mean, God has saved us, so we can save this city. There are other people out there need saving. Now, you join up with us, we're systematic, and we kill VBs."

He didn't demand that you believed anything, just that you fought. It was a nice idea and none of us needed any more convincing. We'd been aimlessly surviving for a few weeks, hiding in corners. Most of us hadn't faced off with one VB yet, and here is this guy leading an army. We wanted to fight back.

He had systems. We'd get into a warehouse, with an escape route set, usually with a vehicle out back or something. Then someone, usually a small fast person, would go outside, until one of the VBs saw them, then they'd run back, we'd be set up in a gauntlet, two rows of armed people, and the VBs would get killed. At first it was kind of amazing.

Pastor John gave sermons about the city after we killed off the VBs. It would be green again. Whatever cancer-causing, tower of Babel technology we'd unleashed that'd brought on the plague, would no longer be used. We'd live a good life, a simple life.

A couple things happened. I hit it off with Jim, because he knew comic books, and Kwanesha because she always said, "Fuck this God shit, but I'm down to kill some crazies." She had a lot of pot, and we'd sneak up to the roof sometimes. One time we were waiting in the warehouse, and the runner popped through the door, and was like, "A lot are coming."

Jim was always in front with the pastor. He was big too. And then eight came through at a time. And the pastor hacked down two, and four got a hold of Jim, and they were falling on him. Jim talked about that moment, seeing them teeth only an inch from his face, holding a whole one in each hand. He said the thing that he hated about that moment is that he might have become one, not that he might stop living. Kwanesha screamed at us, and the rest of us yanked them off Jim, and did them in, but it changed Jim a little. He wasn't that gung ho after that.

But it was the next time we did it, so we're talking maybe only two months into the All Fucked Era, it went crazy. That was when they started with the screeching. At first, the screeching was like a battle cry, but then we realized that it was a call. One would scream, and others would come, and they'd scream too. So there was kind of like a ripple in a pond effect. I mean, us, inside that building, we didn't know what was going on. We'd set up our gauntlet and were beating them to death. This was after guns too. If someone got tired they stepped back, and another came up. I'd taken to using an ax, which was the most common weapon. Try beating someone to death sometime. It takes a lot of effort. But if you can get an ax shot anywhere to the head or neck, it's done.

What happened that time, they screamed and ran in. But they kept coming. It was on my second break that I looked over and saw that there was more dead crazies than there were of us, and that they were coming to the door even harder, even faster. My arms were tired. I had a water blister on the pad of my thumb. The place smelled like blood. That's when I thought about how it worked. Ordinary Wednesday in late May, and where is everybody? Kids are in school. Lots of people in work places. And it was only the loners, or at least the alone, who survived, or stayed sane. The ratios of them, the VBs, to us, had to be astronomical.

I rested until Jim's next break. I said to him, "There is too many. We got to go."

He nodded and grabbed Kwanesha. Nobody noticed us walk out the back. They were too caught up in their mission. Us leaving, it meant something. It wasn't cowardice. We weren't afraid. Jim took his place in that line again even when the VBs almost caught him. Us leaving was saying that there was no hope of killing them off. There were too many. That future green city of Amish farms, that wasn't going to happen. We weren't going to make it.

When Angie said that my hope could be killing them all, I told her that story. She said, "You can hope you find Weapon X: Issue 4." But what I actually hoped was that she'd change her mind.

5. Purpose

I miss video games. I've thought about trying to get to Best Buy. It's four miles. That's a big risk, but if I was sure that all the batteries were still there it might be worth it. The thing is, someone else must have thought of that. Video games were my life. I played a game called *Zombie Apocalypse*. I thought it was fun. In the early days there were a lot of guys who treated AFE like that. They raided gun stores and blasted away. They're all dead now.

Video games have these characters, computer generated, that make it seem like you've got people on your team. Sometimes you talk to them. If you keep staring at the girl in *Zombie Apocalypse*, she calls you a creeper. It's funny. Sometimes you've been playing so long, you forget that actually you're alone, that those voices are just recordings, the characters are just the computer.

Right now, I live to live, and maybe have a little bit of fun. But there is a way in which, alone, I'm not really surviving. One of my teachers had this point, they were talking about a quote from some guy back in the day, "People are social animals." It was something like that. His point was people need people. Now, that teacher probably didn't believe that shit except the animal part. He watched us, knowing we were trying to chew gum, write, "FUCK SCHOOL" on the desks, and check out girls in class. I figured he'd rather be alone in a cave. When I was free, I was alone too, playing video games. I thought those kids were animals too, calling me Lil' Debbie, calling me Toad Chin. I'd love to hear someone call me that now.

They don't talk. They screech, they grunt. They fight each other, not often, and usually not to the death, but they don't talk. If they could talk I wouldn't mind them. I mean, the thing that is the worst about this world is there is no-one to talk to. Even if they were coming at me, trying to kill me, if they were talking, I'd be happy. They could say, "Slow down, lil guy. Toad Chin, where is your chin? Where has it gone? We gone eat you. It'll be fun." That would be cool. Anyway, the VBs are not social. Just animal.

So I'm a social animal, alone. It seems like no-one is left. I haven't seen anybody for seven months. You want to know what happened to Jim, Kwanesha, and the charming (not so much) and beautiful (too much) Angie? I don't want to talk about that.

The strangest thing about the VBs is that sometimes, one of them changes back. It's like a fever, and you've got it, and then you get over it. Lots of people in the beginning changed back from being VBs. I haven't seen it recently, but it happens. They don't usually remember in great detail. They remember running, anger and desire to hunt, not much. They are in rags, their hands are bloody, and they taste blood in their mouths. They usually are pretty upset.

Jim had that happen. He worked in an auto shop, and this crazy guy runs and bites one of his mechanics. Jim runs over there, hits the crazy with a wrench and pins him. The crazy lunges up and bites him on the arm. It hurt like hell, but he didn't know what was happening. Poured some iodine on it, cursed, went back to work. An hour later, he is sick, lying down. Twenty minutes after that and he doesn't remember shit.

The next thing he knows, he's lying down in a backyard. It's a little bit of grass in the middle of a twelve by twelve yard, and he hears screams. Jim had always been an action guy, so he runs down to the street, but pauses. He sees the VBs running. He sees their mouths drenched in blood.

Back then, the most obvious difference between VBs and us was their mouths. If they opened their mouths, you saw bleeding gums. It seems the blood carries the virus. Some people said that the virus makes their mouth bleed. Others said that they chewed on their tongues and cheeks, to bring out the blood. You pick. Either way, their blood goes into your blood and then you're one of them.

Jim paused and watched. He saw them running. He remembered where he'd been last he remembered, his shop, with the crazy guy. And he hid. He only told us that after we'd been together for two months.

Now, I think it happened more at the beginning. People's immune systems, in some cases, fought it off, maybe. But the percents seem to go down, over time. And then there's the problem, what if one of them does change? Now, they're always in packs. And they just kill the recovered. It's like they sense the immunity or something. They don't bother with infection bites. They just eat them. I've seen it.

But I've got a plan. A way to maybe rescue some people.

6. All the Times Jim Saved Me

When I think about my plan, I think about Jim, Kwanesha, and Angie. It was good then. I mean, as good as it ever was in the AFE. I lived with them for eleven months. Well, nine with Angie. Since then, it's been me, VBs, and other enemies. I guess what's hard is, I owe them a lot. I'll start with Jim.

1. When we left Baptist John's Army, we ran out the back door. I was looking back to see that no-one saw us. I almost got bit by a lunger. Jim's two and half feet of wrench caught it in the neck, and you heard this crack like when you pop them package bubbles. Then we had to fight them, 'cause there were a couple. I figure we saved the Baptist Army too, 'cause they were only looking for the VBs to come from one side.

2. On a forage run, I lay down in a bed. A VB came out from under the bed while I was sleeping (ambush!). I was two seconds from bit, asleep, when Jim jumped up (we were all in the same bed. It was winter. It's also much safer to be in the same room, as this story shows) and grabbed it around the neck. I wasn't really awake yet and he was already on the floor, cutting off its air supply with his thick ass fingers, while the VB made gurgles. I sort of looked from bed, mainly thinking I was still dreaming. These kinds of dreams happen a lot in the AFE.

3. I was taking a dump and they attacked that house. Jim tip toe raced up the stairs and told me, even though there was an escape on the first floor, into the next

house. He said, "They're at the front and back. It stinks in here. Let's go."

"I got to wipe my ass!"

"No time," and he was gone. I'm not going to tell you the rest of the story but I will say that nobody's personal hygiene was the same in the AFE.

4-23. We were in about twenty fights we'd have lost without Jim. We won them.

24. Jim invented the theory of five exits. That really saved me a lot of times.

25. Jim taught us how to cook with the sun.

26. Jim treated me like a person. Maybe a son.

Nice memories, right? But they just make me guilty.

7. Kwanesha, My Kung Fu Master

Maybe you thought when you read how I killed VBs, this dude is on some no joke the real post-apocalyptic true G shit. That's how I like to think about myself, like I just don't give a fuck and if you fuck with me, you're dead. It isn't true. I'm really cautious and stay inside, in rooms with five exits and re-read comic books. I go out only because eating is necessary and then I'm real cautious. I go room to room, tree to tree, listening for VBs. If I hear them I lay low 'til they're gone. I might take half a day to go half a block to get to that Quik-Stop.

But there was a time when I couldn't even take the necessary risk. Like imagine you're on a plane (those don't exist anymore) and someone says the engine failed and the plane is going to crash and burn. Everybody has to jump out with parachutes. And then you're like "No, I won't jump." That's dumb, right? But that was me. I was scared of everything.

Even back in Baptist John's Army, they'd be coming through the door, and I'd be like, "Oh, shit!" and do nothing. Not moving. Fortunately I was surrounded by guys who believed it was their duty to make a difference and kill those things. It was Kwanesha who saw me, who saw that I didn't take the necessary risks.

"You're from the hood, right?"

"Yeah."

"How come you act like such a pussy?"

"What do you mean?"

"Bitch ass pussy." And she slapped me. She was just as big as me, and way meaner so I didn't do anything. She stared at me, real hard, and I looked away. Then she slapped me again as hard she could. I fell on my ass.

I had the sweetest Mom in the world. She brought me Lil Debbies and hot dogs, already prepared how I like them, relish, ketchup and mustard (just saying that makes me so hungry I could turn into a VB), mashed potatoes, chicken nuggets. I could play Xbox, and not have to move. She washed my clothes. I could cuss somebody out in a school yard, but I didn't get in no fights. When the kids started calling me Toad Chin I cut school. My mom didn't know 'cause she was working. Which is say, I was from the hood, but not like Kwanesha. I stayed inside to avoid people and life. I cut school. As far as I was concerned life could be all video games. Kwanesha was real street, true G, actually-didn't-give-a-fuck. She said what she thought, and she wasn't scared of anyone.

I didn't say anything, and she started laughing at me. She said to Jim, "Look at this pussy."

We were alone, up on the roof. It'd been a bloody day. Jim was working some kind of alcohol and me and Kwanesha had smoked a joint. Jim said, "Go easy on the kid."

She said, "Easy? You think these streets are going to be easy on him?" As if to emphasize this, a shriek came from the street, sounding like teeth sharp flesh hunger.

Kwanesha went on. "He gone get eaten alive. VB hors d'oeuvres and shit." She slapped me again and this time it stung so bad I jumped up and pushed her. "Jim, you see this? He pushed me. Oh, well now I'm real intimidated. I won't do this again." And to demonstrate 'this' she faked a slap with her right and in response to my flinch hammered me with a left-handed ear-popping, thunder-slap. This time I got up, so mad I didn't think about her being tougher than me, trying to hit her. She blocked each flailing arm, interspersing that with slaps of her own. While I tried to hit her, she kept talking. "Oh, now maybe I won't slap you again. It's getting to be work, not hard work, but work, to keep you from getting revenge."

I still had some chub and I stopped, out of breath after about five minutes. She sat down across the roof and smiled. "Hey," she said, "I'm a teach you how to fight, pussy."

I'm a thinking person. Not the smartest or anything, but I look at things. And I figured that Kwanesha was telling me that if I didn't stick up for myself, she was going to keep slapping me. That was just an example of life. If I didn't like it, I had to do something- take necessary risks. If she hadn't taught me that, as well as how to fight, I would not have lived to today.

The guy I am now, the calm I feel when those things are lunging at me with their bloody mouth, she taught me that. The strength to fight back, I owe her more than I owe Jim.

8. Fighting to the Death for Fun

I get my head twisted, thinking about the past, when what it's about is survival. This isn't a world for pussies, right. It's a world for people who always keep one hand on a weapon. When it's time to use it, they are silent, and efficient. You spend too much time thinking you don't think at all.

So when I was in that reverie, writing about the past, they came. I didn't hear them until one was trying my door. Back before Kwanesha's lessons, I'd have sat down and quietly shit my pants, waited for them to break through the door, and allowed their blood-wet teeth to infect me, and joined the VBs. But I'm ready now- though I'd be a lot more ready if I'd paid attention to the ringing bells I've set up. The bells are connected to strings and when someone enters the house they ring. I was so deep in the memory of Kwanesha's slaps . . .

They're outside the bedroom door. It's bolted three times. I've got a few minutes depending on how many are out there. I peek through the blinds, not touching them. There are more on the street, looking around. Then the one of the group at the door screeches. The VBs outside twitch, orienting on my room. So much for that exit.

Jim made a theory. It's called The Theory of Five Exits. One of the things that changed is the VBs got smarter. They never talked but they developed their own language. Screeches, grunts, pushes. Bared teeth. They had the same goal, so that cuts out the need for a lot of communication.

When we were leaving that Baptist Slaughter House was one of the first times we saw it. They started hunting like wolves, circling you, chasing you into ambushes. It made escape terrifying and a lot of people didn't catch onto the transition. They thought it was all run faster than them, and they didn't realize until they got tackled from the front and the teeth were going in, the virus tingling in their blood. We realized it and Jim said we have to have multiple exits. After three exits wasn't really enough of a margin, (we had a couple of close calls) Jim started saying you needed five.

I already told you there is the hall door, and the window. I have two trap doors, carefully disguised, going up and going down. But they are probably filling the house now and I can't risk that one. The fifth is pretty smart, and it wouldn't have worked back when I was a fatty. I'd cut into the main duct work, that used to go to the furnace. I'd cut it open in the basement as well.

I lower my travel pack down, and then myself, moving slowly and smoothly. For all I know they are in the living room, and if they hear me they could rip out the wall, and break up that duct work like a candy wrapper getting to the chocolaty goodness of me. I hear them breathing, grunting, moving furniture. A loud banging starts, and I know they are breaking down the door into my room. I unload into the basement, landing on my toes, lowering myself out of the duct work without a sound. There is one VB, youngish, looking back up the stairs. I pull Ackee off my back and swing hard, burying the main point in its skull. Not even a squeak from him. I move up and catch the body, lowering it onto the floor. Rest in peace, at least you aren't hungry no more.

Meanwhile the crashing is turning into the sound of wood breaking. The second they realize I'm not in the room, they are going to spread out searching for me. I go under the basement stairs, where I've dug a hole into the neighboring basement. I crawl through, and shove a piece of plywood over the hole. There are two of these holes, and so I'm two houses away when I hear the screeches that signal they know they lost me. By then, I'm shimmying into an eighteen inch wide hole I've dug in the front of the basement. Behind me I pull a fitted plug into this hole. This cap is made of concrete, and blends with the wall. In the tunnel it's pitch black, and cramped, but this is a necessary risk. I used to be scared of rats.

If they get the plague, I won't live long though, regardless of whether I crawl into the sewers. That is where my hole goes. It delivers me into an egg shaped tunnel, two feet high, eighteen inches wide, and I crawl along this. I'm claustrophobic, everyone is. We're not moles.

I breathe deep, and think, necessary risk. Or I think, now I'm on some true G shit. Kwanesha would be proud.

31

9. Angie Again

It's easier to say to someone you wouldn't be with them, even if they were the last person on earth, than it is to actually reject them at the end of time. What happened was we sat around, while Kwanesha and Jim made sure that whenever they died or went VB, they'd be able to say that at least they had an orgasm in the past hour.

"Do they ever get tired?" she asked.

I shrugged because I didn't think they did, but sometimes I think they just lay together naked. Enjoying being that close. I told some jokes. We'd watch through a tinted window the parade of VBs. One came by, naked. This became how they lived. At some point, they were like," I eat people. The fuck I need clothes for?" I'd ask her, one naked one came by, his body lean like a cheetah, his mouth hanging open like a hyena, "What about that guy? You date him?"

It was funny, in a dumb way.

I was considerate because she was beautiful. I prepared the meals for everyone. It was usually baked beans and sun-cooked rice, something out of a can. Bread was gone by then, eaten by mold. I would tell her stories about being made fun of in high school. "They called me toad chin."

"I can see why."

"You shouldn't say things like that when you're hot. It's not fair. I wish I had a chin like yours." I tapped her chin, Irish lil square.

She rolled her eyes at this, but there was the hint of a smile on her face. She liked the fact that her cuteness still mattered to someone. I knew it wasn't me, except for maybe my humanness, but I kept it up.

One day, in the shitload of time we lived in, my life changed. That's what I hate about zombie movies. Everything is always exciting. But in the real thing, the ALL FUCKED ERA, there is a lot of quiet, and hiding. Reading books in a whisper to the last living girl. She came across the room and sat on the couch. Her leg was naked, it was summer, and her thigh touched mine. I looked over at her but she just told me to keep reading. I was reading *The Hunger Games*. That's how bored we were. We read books. I preferred *Harry Potter*, but we'd read all of those twice. The *Hunger Games* never makes you laugh, but Harry got jokes.

"Would you like to kiss me," she asked.

"I'm trying to read," I said. I didn't think there was any chance she meant it. Black eyes, dark hair, pale skin. Her legs had hair on them. Come on. You think we had water to waste on shaving? I thought it looked good. They were a nice little shape. I had no chance.

I kept reading, and then she leaned toward me but I ignored it because it couldn't be real but then I felt her cool lips play along my neck and I knew it was real.

"Kiss me back, weirdo."

We kissed. I learned as I went. It was nice. She said, "You know it doesn't mean anything. I just wanted to thank you for reading."

I said, "Well, it means you lied when you said there was no chance."

She laughed. "You still have no chance; it's just harder for you to believe that now."

She really meant it. I saw that not only was the fact that I was the only guy she knew on my side, but sheer boredom was working with me. After that, and I'd never know when, she'd make out with me. I wasn't at Jim and Kwanesha levels of happiness, but to me it seemed that death was a little less scary, now that I could say I'd kissed a girl. Or she'd kissed me. Even that freak Georgy Porgy kissed girls, though they all cried.

10. Plan

So life became boring. After Jim, Kwanesha and Angie were gone, I mean. Not like a little boring. Like, I'm about to fucking crush my head with a concrete block boring. I realize that it's 'cause I'm alone and that man is a social beast. I'm not satisfied living alone.

But really I had a whole other reason which was way more complicated, but I can't tell you about that. I'm working up to it. That reason is the one that makes me do it- because it involves more than necessary risk.

Part of the plan was to find some people for myself. I already told you that the VBs sometimes come out of it. They look around, and it's like, "What the fuck is going on?" Like when a sleepwalker wakes up, or a possessed person gets unpossessed.

The thing is, and I've seen this multiple times, the other VBs know. Most times it's kind of obvious when a pack of naked humans are hunting, and one stops and looks around with an expression like, "Why are you guys naked? Why is there blood on your teeth? Shouldn't we cook that squirrel before we eat it?"

What would you do? You'd cry, and scream, maybe run, maybe fight. You wouldn't just keep marching along like everything is okay. So the VBs know pretty quick, and they go for this person so fast, so vicious. They always kill them and eat them all the way. It's fucking terrible to see. One second you wake up in this city, broken worse than Humpty Dumpty, nobody can put it back to together again, and the next second you're being eaten alive. They never bite these people with an infecting bite. No. Kill them. Eat them.

Jim said he thought he was immune, because he already had it. He thought that was why they killed them. They knew the come-to people were immune.

There was one guy at the Baptist Army who told a story about it. He woke up and he was sleeping in a pile of raggedy humans. There was a smell. It was the human animal. Sweat, sex, dirt. He felt really weird but he was so disoriented he didn't move. He watched. And the others started stirring. Scratching themselves, stretching. He copied them. He was waiting for someone to say something, "Good orgy. See you next time." But they didn't, just looked around with sullen eyes, and then a big one grunted and they all started following him. This guy, the one who came too, just jumps in. They went about two blocks before they started chasing someone. He fell behind, freaked out but what was happening. He could taste blood in his mouth. But one dropped back, a female that was kind of fat. She turned to him, while the others were hunting and sniffed. Then she screeched. He's still bewildered, but he's also scared as fuck, and when she did this he started jogging away. Good thing to, because in a second the VBs were chasing him. He ran. He said all the physical work-out of being a VB helped him because even though he was gassed, he could keep running.

He went down streets, up streets. The fat one dropped back but there were a couple others. So he killed them. He was real awake then, no more sleepy time. Like I said, he was in the Baptist Army.

36

He was also a story teller. But that one, I believed.

The point is, people needed an opportunity to come out of it in safety. If you could get them isolated, as VBs from the pack, there was a chance. That's the plan.

Now you're saying, what are the odds? And I'm asking that. Because lots of people came out of it at the beginning, but I haven't seen it happen recently. Of course, I'm not on the streets except for food and forage runs. And then, how many would I have to have, in isolation, before one came out of it? It might never happen.

And then I'd keep living as before.

I picture a building. Something big with lots of rooms, I can lock them in there. And watch. The day they say, "Help?" I'll have a friend. Of course, right now, I'm snugged into a sewer listening to them screech and smash through my carefully constructed den. It's going to take some work.

11. Angie's Kindness

She was small but feisty. Black Irish. She had a lot of stories about the few months she survived on her own. Back then you had a lot of options. The Baptist Army, different groups. Team up with somebody. Sometimes they fought one another. Mostly they survived.

But Angie didn't join any of them. Girls were treated kind of shitty then. Some guys were like, I'll protect you but you got to serve me. Some girls killed guys. Lots of guys killed girls. There wasn't any law, and even people that was kind of good had no time to look around and help someone else.

Mostly she hid. She had that little league bat, and a couple of knives, and she hid in sewers, garbage cans, and under beds. The VBs found her often. They've got a good sense of smell. When they came into the bedroom, and looked under the bed, she stabbed them in the eyes. She swung her little league bat like crazy.

She killed her share of VBs. I remember we tried to count once, but when we got only ten days in to our memories of the All Fucked Era, we'd both gotten twenty, so we figured we'd never remember all of them. Jim said he killed some exact number, one thousand three hundred some. I think he might have counted some of Baptist John's, though.

At first, she kissed me because there was nothing else to do. Then she kissed me because she liked me, not in a sexual way, but as a person, and she knew I'd appreciate it. Then she figured that kissing a loser who was alive and not crazy was better than nothing. I mean, at some point, it's not really true that you wouldn't be with someone if they were the last person on earth. You would be with anybody- I don't want to go too far into this, because you might freak out, but you can kiss your belief in gender, or what's too old, or even who's too close of a relative, goodbye. At the end of the world anyone is better than being alone. I remember when we read mythology it was like, at first, people had to marry sisters and brothers to make it work.

So maybe it wasn't such a surprise that after a month of heating her meals in the sun cooker Jim made, reading her *The Hunger Games* and *Harry Potter*, she started sleeping with me. But she started out to do it as an act of charity. She put a lot of effort into kissing. You looked at her and figured she was the kind of girl that never kissed half way, but I never really believed that she was that into it with me. She kind of sighed and grunted before the first time she grabbed my hand and led me to the couch. Now I think she was getting over her disgust for me.

That might sound a little harsh on me. I've had a lot of time to think this through. I was the kind of guy who makes jokes about sex because he knows nothing about it. Girls feel awkward around that kind of guy, because he's so clearly into them but he doesn't say anything that lets them know, and he's trying to be something he's not, and he doesn't like himself either. The only reason I had a chance with her was because she teamed up with us, and I had enough time, like weeks, to get over being nervous and weird, and then too, she was nice.

I suppose that should be a bad memory. She had to steel herself in order to have sex with me. It's not though. To me it's like, she loved me that much. She did that for me.

I guess what it's working around to, all these memories, is one big thing. But before I get there I want to say that those three people loved me. Jim was kind, and saved my life. Kwanesha was my kung fu master. Angie was my only love. Out of charity. They should have had that. Like total loser guys can get a social worker who provides them with special services to help them meet girls. I guess that's what prostitutes are for. You're saying, terrible. But you haven't lived here. If I could sell sex and walk down the street without fearing VB, I'd do it. Of course, ho was never a safe job.

I was a sixteen year old boy at the end of the world. The only woman I knew of was with another guy that I couldn't compete with. I was resigned to my only lover being my hand. Then Angie loved me.

Balled up in the eighteen inch sewer pipe, my bag of essentials connected to me by a rope, I cry for myself that I had Angie and I lost her. I cry for Angie.

12. Warehouses vs. Apartment buildings

How intelligent are the VBs? I don't know. Sometimes very. For instance, they found my room. Tucked away in the egg-sewer, I know that they are trashing it, ripping through the comics, bending and blunting my weapons. It's fine. I had the important stuff packed in this one bag, and Ackee is with me. They do this so that I can't come back, so I'll have to run. That's what I think anyway.

It comes down to this question. Say you were trying to run a prison with one guard, and crazy wild cannibals as inmates. Your pick of facilities. Where would you go? An apartment building? Here the problem is that you can't really monitor your inmates. You stick them in the rooms, and then you don't know what they get up to. And while VBs normally don't use tools, what might happen if I left them like that? They could dig through plaster walls. They could kill themselves trying to bang through a wall with their head.

Some warehouses are better. You know the kind where the boss walks around on an elevated walkway. That way, I could be up there, and watch them all. Shoot them if necessary. The problem there is, I kind of need them separate so that if one turns the others don't rip them apart. It'd be like all that work for nothing. So then I'm building all those walls on the floor of the warehouse. Strong walls that VBs can't climb equals a lot of work.

I think it goes without saying that this is a suicide mission. Up to now, I've learned to survive and that is all about being quiet and quick, and occasionally killer. It's about creating good odds. But the VBs will screech like crazy when I catch them. I will have to use a vehicle to transport them. That will bring more. That's why I figure guns as part of the plan. I mean, it will be nice if one of them comes out of it, and I get some help, but it isn't so likely.

I have to look out in the suburbs. There was a lower density of VBs out there. So, probably a warehouse. I could build walls in it, so I could watch from above but they couldn't see each other. I will have to be able to make it secure from the inside, and outside. I'll have to be able to monitor to pull out any that turned back, and to break up anything. It sounds difficult, I know.

It is odd, to me, that I will be settling in for so much work. I know I won't be great at it, though I learned some basics of building from Jim and a few more things from having to construct my hideouts. At the same time, this is the human race I am trying to save. Before the All-Fucked Era, I didn't care that much about humans.

My mom was nice, but I never saw my dad. The rest of them were mean. I was kind of happy when everybody turned into VBs. It just their real them, the I-will-do-anything-to-get-ahead attitude. Now they would eat me, but before, calling my Toad Chin, it was pretty much the same.

Now. Well, like I said. I owe the human race a little. Hell. I owe them my life. So I will try to save it. I know, right. Former fat kid as the human race's last hope. Kind of seems like we've fallen on hard times.

13. Flashback

The human race, back before AFE, wasn't something I gave a fuck about. I mean, when this happened, and people started ripping the flesh off one another, I kind of thought it was just the same old. People did that to my little twelve year old heart, "Yo, Toad Face, how come you got volcanoes on your face." Times like this, feelings don't matter, but then, it was all I had. Like I could do anything about how my face was. People always were a vicious kind.

It's kind of weird that it took most of the human race going animal, for me to fall in love with it. You know where I'm going. I'm talking about Jim, Kwanesha, and Angie. My make-shift family. I already went on about what they did, and all the stuff they did for me. When I look a VB in the eye, and I don't feel any fear but think about what I need to do, that's Kwanesha. And when I breathe, that's Jim. And when I know I'm a man, somehow, and I don't know why, worthy of love, that's Angie.

Where are they now, Toad Chin? If you like them so much?

It was a quiet day. The VBs had been changing, and we knew some things, like the screeching and how they all ran when they heard it. But the stalking, we were a little slow on that. Jim and Kwanesha were taking a little rest from their normal activities and hanging downstairs with us. We were playing Monopoly. Really, if you are at the end of the world, and you don't have electricity, and you are trying to waste a lifetime, that's your game. It sucked, especially compared to *Zombie Apocalypse*, but the company was good.

Angie was gloating 'cause she'd locked up Boardwalk and Park Place. Kwanesha had just landed on it and she was cursing Angie out as she paid rent. Jim was smiling like he was Santa and we were kids opening presents.

We heard a slam at the front door, and then lots of banging. Jim peeked out there. He said, "There's a bunch. Screaming. Kwanesha, help me out. Angie, get the packs. TC, you check the back door." He always had Kwanesha fight by him. He said that he was going to die before her, because there was no point in living if she was done. Kwanesha said, "I like you, Jim, but my goal is to survive this bitch." She didn't mean it though. It would take a real selfish person to abandon their family in the hour of need.

He'd already unsheathed his long wrench, the thing weighed about twenty pounds, but in his hands it whirled like a cheerleader's baton. I shouldn't talk about cheerleaders. It's weird for horniness to make to make you sad.

I ran to the back door. As I was getting there, I heard the front door crash open, and a wall of grabbing, biting VBs surged through it. I saw that long wrench slamming into them, but I didn't think he could fight out of that one. Out the back, there was one VB, screeching. I could see others running across the back lot to join him, and in a minute Jim and Kwanesha would go down, and I'd be next.

I could run out the back, kill the one, and live, or try and fight it out with the others (and die).

14. Obvious, Terrible

Well, you know the rest, right? I'm still here. They're not. I say I don't want to talk about it, but really it's the only thing I think about so it's sort ridiculous to say that. When I think about it, I get all tight in the stomach. How come the things you hate thinking about are the only things you think about?

So I said I am alive, they are dead. It makes it sound like if I helped, I'd be dead. And the odds were like that, but they weren't a hundred to one. They were nineteen to one, that with my help, we'd have made it. Bad odds, but in hindsight . . . Hindsight is bullshit. This is a record of a former pimple faced warrior and his fucked up head at the end of the world. What you see looking at the past, you think you understand what it means, but you don't really know. That's why I keep thinking about it.

I ran down the stairs. I pulled aside the plywood that hid the hole, slid through the hole, and pulled the sheet back in place. Sometimes I believe this, the pulling the sheet back to block the hole, more than the running, was the worst thing. I knew they weren't going to make it. I hadn't even shouted where I was going. I knew that outside was crawling with the hungry ones, so I jumped in a hidey hole in the basement. I could hear the fight through the floors and plywood. Screaming, Angie's high pitched, Kwanesha's roaring, and Jim silent except for the smack of his long wrench breaking bones. Not once did I rethink my position. I thought, "What are the chances the VBs don't find me here?" Then Kwanesha stopped

46

roaring, and Angie stopped screaming. Still the long wrench smacked, POP, POP.

Now Jim began to curse, "You fucking piece of shit virus beasts." POP POP. "You let her get killed, you big fuck up." This was to himself. "Kwanesha's down," I thought. Pop. POP.

After he stopped cursing it went on for a while, just the solitary POP. I knew he'd been bitten by then, but he kept fighting. The virus didn't take, which is like chicken pox or something. He'd already had it. They couldn't kill him. Then the weeping. At first I thought he was laughing, that he'd gone over the edge, because it was loud, and donkey like, and then I realized it was weeping, because he was saying "TC, Angie. Kwanesha. My lil Neesh." And stuff like that. Then more loud donkey noises. All the while the POP POP of his long wrench.

Of course this is interspersed with their snarling-screeching, and then the POPs stopped and it was just the sound of flesh crunching between teeth.

You might say something like, well, you shouldn't feel bad. You were in shock. I wasn't. I knew all about the VBs. I wasn't scared of them, not shock scared. I went into that hole just to live to another day. If I'd have known how poor my life would become, alone, I'd have tried to save them. But that's not really different. That's just me trying to take care of myself a different way.

I got out of the hole twenty four hours later. It was totally quiet, Silent Night type of shit, but I didn't feel peaceful inside. I crawled back through the slot and investigated. I found one set of bones. From the ripped apart purple t-shirt confettied around the rest of the room, and the height of the skeleton I knew it was Jim. I looked for a corpse of Angie or Kwanesha, but didn't find them. It looked like they'd joined the VBs.

Then a terrible thought struck me, that Kwanesha had time to turn while Jim fought. In the end, he was probably unable to fight because he was looking at her face. Actually, being eaten by her was probably what he wanted.

I thought about burying his bones but it seemed melodramatic and bullshitty 'cause if I actually cared I'd have done something about it when it happened, if him dying meant that much. In the end I just moved on. Looked for other people. Then I found out that there weren't any.

At least they don't hold it against me. Jim thought I died. Everyone else is dead. The only person left to judge me is myself. Of course, I'm good at that, tougher than a District Attorney. See, it's easy to regret now. I know I was losing some of the LAST people. At the time I thought I could start over with some new people. It's all about ME. That's why I'm glad I'm alone. I deserve to be alone. It's just that my family didn't deserve to die.

My mission, a VB farm, where I monitor them, try to save the ones that turn, I figure it's a low survival percentage mission. And I thought of that plan a long time ago, but I was like, that plan is too hard. Especially for one person. Too risky. But the longer I thought, the more it came down to, I'm a lil pussy who let my fam die- if I get eaten by some VBs- fine. Good. That's the shit a piece of shit like myself deserves.

15. Zoo?

They've got a lot of names. VBs. Viral beasts. That was what one scientist called them, in the first few days and it stuck. I've heard them called wolf-men, The Enraged, and the soulless. Blood mouths. I believe that I am the foremost expert on their behavior living. Of course, I'm the foremost expert on everything 'cause everyone else is dead.

What else about them? They have some kind of intelligence. I've heard the theory, from survivors, back when there were some, that each VB didn't serve itself, or its hunger, but that they served the virus. Like they will more often than not bite a victim, gnashing their teeth and bloody gums into them, and then not eat them. The victim has only a short time, depending on the person, between fifteen minutes to three hours, before he's a VB too.

That intelligence is the problem with trying to capture them. It's a big complication. I thought long and hard about where to put them. I need to be able to isolate them, and monitor them. I started thinking about prisons. That is what a prison is, right?

What about the zoo? It's the same thing, except for animals, and it's closer. I start creeping south house to house. I avoid a few packs, just lay low, when I run into something that you don't see too much. It is a pack, and out in front of it is a dog. A VB dog. I get low in the house I'm in, just ducked down so none of them would see me, but then I hear him bark a couple times.

Most animals realized that people had turned crazy and they ran for it. They got away. Some, usually dogs, didn't catch the change. You know dogs. They love people no matter what. Just imagine poor Blackie running up to his master, wagging his tail- and then he gets bit.

Those dogs turned into VB dogs. I'd only seen a few when we were with the Baptist Army. What they did was they came at you, super hard. They also could sniff you out way better than humans. Of course, we weren't really hiding when we were in the Baptist Army. We waited for them and we killed- so we were ready when barking dogs came through the door.

When we were waiting there, baiting them, fully armed, there was usually a person in reserve. Usually a smaller person or a less fit person, like myself. I was still chunky then. That person was armed with a gun, and anytime the fight got crazy they were to fire. The rule was, the second a dog comes in, shoot them. They are too fast to go hand to hand combat.

Jim also said to me once, "If the human VBs are hunting you, you evaluate. You look at your chances, and if they're okay, you fight. If they're bad, try to run away and hide. If a dog is after you, you got to kill that fucker. He can smell you no matter what, so there isn't any hiding." I kind of hoped it never came down to that.

The dog is barking, getting closer to the window, I can tell by the volume. I already got Ackee out, in my hand. The window is got no glass so he's going to come right in. I stand up, figuring I want to get a good swing, and human

VBs know, from this thing's barking, that a normal human is here. No use hiding. He's big, some kind of German Shepherd, and as he comes up the steps I see his teeth, blood-drenched, virus ridden, snapping with each bark, and then he's flying through the window.

I swing too early, too nervous. He sees the many tines of Ackee flying at him and twists in the air. It is weird, like this thing turned in midair. He lands, squares toward me. Snarling, darting forward and back. I'm shitting my pants 'cause I know his human buddies are seconds away. We circle there, in the row home living room, jumping over broken chairs, slipping on magazines about how to go on a diet and dye your hair red, until my back is toward the stairs. I back up them, Ackee out jabbing at the snarling dog.

He leaps at me. I meet his teeth with a stabbing motion from Ackee, but 'cause the weapon was already out in front of me, I don't get much weight behind it. He's not hurt. In fact, the only difference is that now more blood is pouring out from his mouth, and if anything, he's angrier, his snarling filling the house, his body low toward the stairs, cocked like a pistol about to fire.

I have to act now; time is not on my side. I hear them piling through the windows below, shrieking. I lift Ackee to get a proper swing. He springs. His teeth are inches from my belly. I bring my knee up, hard into his chest. As he twists in the air, I bring down Ackee. It catches and buries in his hind-section. No babies for this hound. Then I bring it up, as his legs thump onto the stairs and hammer it into his head.

A male human VB is charging up the stairs. "Come on, blood-face!" I slam Ackee accurately, with one swing. He tumbles down. Philly row-home stairs are narrow, and this gives me a second. I run down the second floor hall toward the back room. It's got a window, glass still in.

Oh well.

I run and leap into it. Full commitment- CRASH- tinkle tinkle. I land going into a roll. Hoping not to injure an ankle. Seems okay, and I'm up. They'll be after me. I leap fences, and find a house with a basement to hole up. They screech around for a while, give up, go back and eat the dog and the man.

As I'm hiding, I think about the zoo. And I think what if- right, a hyena got bit? They're locked in cages, they got nowhere to run. Those hyenas can bite through anything. Or worse. A lion. Me and Ackee vs. a lion, with the virus? I'm not going to win. An elephant? Imagine being chased by an elephant with a virus. Those things can run thirty miles an hour, and throw trees. Of course, could an elephant bite you? Maybe they got blood on the tusks. Those are technically teeth, you know.

So when I thought about all that, I decided to stay away from the zoo.

.

16. Holmesburg

I had this seventh grade math teacher. Thought he was a tough guy, took us on a field trip to Holmesburg. Check it out kids. Hallways spoked off a center hub, each hallway lined with cells. A massive three story wall around the place. "You act a fool, this is where you'll be," teach said. "Or someplace like it." I looked around, thought about the joints I smoked, the video games I played. Yeah, whatever. It didn't seem scary, and it didn't seem lonelier than my life.

It was the perfect place to become a jailer for blood-mouths, to wait, against all hope for one of them to maybe turn back.

It's a journey up there. The streets are almost empty, only occasional packs of VBs less interested in me than rats. The blood-faces may be seeing what I'm seeing. There are no people left. If there are no people there is nothing to hunt. Will they start hunting one another?

A group of blood-faces come by while I'm walking a block of row homes on the roof. That way I can see. I drop down and watch them. SHIT. I think it's Angie, the hair color is right. It's a small VB too. Then I see the jaw; it's a hard line. Not her. The face. Not her. But I'm shaking and then I fall down on the roof and wish I believed in praying to say I was sorry. Sorry, Angie. Sorry, VB that's not Angie. Stop being a little bitch, TC. You got shit to do.

The prison is the same fucked up place. I don't notice the loneliness because that's everywhere, until I start reading the walls. Stuff my twelve year old self didn't see but I see it now. I see it because it's humans trying to say something. Humans talking to nobody.

I wish Alisha was here.

A lot of things about wanting pussy. That was lonely too.

A picture, careful details, rear view mirrors, wheel wells, the swerving lines of a Corvette. Must have been a lot of work drawing on these pocked walls. He was saying, "I love life. I love fucking beautiful cars. I miss seeing them move."

Another type of scrawl was the confessional. These are low, where they could be hidden behind bed frames. *I didn't see the kid there. Motherfucker. Why a kid there?*

I'm sorry, mama. I fucked up. He couldn't say it to her. I guess that's why he wrote it on the wall, an unsaid confession, shit that would never be forgiven.

I feel an echo through time. These men wanting to speak to someone so hard, to say some shit like, I love cars, I love pussy, I love Malik. Not able to speak they wrote it on the walls, and nobody cared, until I came here.

I hear it 'cause I'm not that different. I carry some shit for which there is no forgiveness, because all the priests, every human who could either say, "That shit is terrible, but we all do bad shit," or "It's okay," is gone. I'd even take, "Even though you are terrible, I like you anyway."

A writing on another wall. I've lost track of time because these voices, these wall scribbles make me feel like I am hearing a human voice.

Worse than dragons, the many tearings of the end!

Not one thousand lions, not a million hyenas, the breaking of all.

God. NO. NO NO. Hold BACK.

He listens not.

The END cometh, cometh, COMETH!!!

These scrawlings are the shape of wolf teeth, savagely slashed in crayon.

I bet the guards and the inmates hated the writer. "Crazy Bob, shut the fuck up. We're trying to sleep."

"I see the end," he screams. "All is going to end." They punch him, but he still speaks. They stick him in solitary, but he still sees. Still cries out. He knew about the blood mouths, the All Fucked Era. Weird shit.

I put U-locks and stuff on the gates and prison cell doors, it takes some days. Walking around I feel their ghosts, the men who fought for their freedom and died in the riots, and the men who fought for order and justice and died in the riots. I like the haunting. Talk to me in my sleep, dead men. At least it's conversation.

I need that shit.

17. Last Worker in Animal Control

I'm not going to tell you all about the U-Locks and the chains, and the stockpiled duct tape and handcuffs. Just think what you would do if you were making an old, rusty prison for humans treated like animals, into a prison for human animals. I did that, but better than you, because you don't know blood mouths the way I know them. You got to live through this shit to become the well-oiled machine, the duct tape technician, that I am.

Anyway, I had to catch a VB. That was the whole plan, to catch them and hold them, in the hopes they'd shake out of it like I'd seen them do sometimes. Each time that happened, the pack around them turned on them, and devoured them. I move out into the city. I'm in the Northeast blocks, no rows of houses with connected roofs. Instead you got individual houses, separated by driveways. No roof walking here. Got to navigate on the ground between houses, among the rolling trash cans. I watch one pack for a while. They have a house that they live in. The doorway is battered and finger marked, like a mouse hole. The human smell oozes out of the house and sneaks down my nostrils. Disgusting.

Every day the pack swings out, some fast ones jogging in front, the big ones in the middle, the small ones spread around them. Like a wolf pack. There is a little one that I think I could corral. He's dark haired, with girl eyes; he looks like a baby deer. I wait until they are sleeping. I tip toe up to the window, deep snoring coming from the glassless hole. I see flesh on flesh, a mound of human,

57

rising and falling like one body. I back away slow. I'm not going to extract one of them from that pile.

More likely to get one while they are hunting. They tend to chase squirrels, and deer, which they eat, instead of turning them. Good thing, too. I think a deer chasing me is scarier than an elephant. Right? They jump eight foot fences like nothing, melt into the trees like ninjas. Course, VBs are no slouches themselves. They spend half the day running, their faces low to the ground like dogs smelling for piss.

Next time the pack shambles out, I'm watching. There are eighteen and I don't follow them 'til I count the last one. Don't want them lifting up the screech for me. He lags a little, the small pretty one. Awesome. I trot silently behind. He urinates while running, his hand wiping the stuff off his leg. He's going fast. Twenty yards ahead a larger female turns occasionally, growling at him, like he's in trouble. I wait until she rounds a corner on a house, and then I'm on him. As he turns, I bring the handle end of Ackee across his cheek. He goes down. He's light and young. Must have been eleven when the viru-pocalypse ignited.

I wrap his face with duct tape fast. Then I drag him as he comes to toward some bushes. He is still half conscious, and I latch cuffs onto his arms, and cinch my legs around his while I grind his face against the dirt.

The female is back; she looks around the corner, and lets out a bark, a note of question at the end. The pretty VB is all the way awake, struggling against me, trying to respond to the bark. I push harder, plowing his small face

58

into the mulch that some happy grandmom put down two years ago, thinking about the house looking nice for the grandkids. The female starts forward, another bark. If she stays another two moments I have to run. She'll see me, and let up the screech. Com'on, bitch. Back to the hunt.

Maybe I'm developing powers of mind control. I don't know. She turns and trots off, back toward the pack. Their behavior can be as erratic as a cat, and she must assume he's hunting a rat. There hasn't been anyone hunting VBs for a while. The Baptist Army . . . okay, that one is for another day.

I sling him atop my shoulder. "Com'on, Foxy," I think. "I'm taking you home." I'm pretty fit, and I manage a jog with him across my shoulders. He must weigh under a hundred pounds so it could be worse. Back to Holmesburg.

I have a special cell for him, the one that belonged to the prophet of the apocalypse. What I think is that there once was a guy in this cell who saw the truth, sense, when nobody else could. He saw this coming. I'm hoping his ghost is around and it can coach Foxy into understanding again, when everyone else has lost all sense (except me).

I drop him in the cell, and point out one of the scrawls.

Will heaven open again?
Will the fire rain stop, the black blanket of death lift.
In my dreams beyond the end I see. I SEE.
But all must be eaten, chewed up and swallowed, the beast that comes.

"See that," I said. "Some hope there, right?"

He looked at me, his pretty eyes almost seemed intelligent. His eyes seem to say, "I don't know. That could mean a lot of things, TC." Then he got up and ran into the wall, banging it with his head. "Shit," I said. Blood is trickling out of his curly hair. I chain him to a ring I'd affixed to the middle of the floor. I get a pair of scissors and cut the hair close, and look at the cut. Not bad. I work it with peroxide, which he appreciates. I put a bandaid on it. His jaw works against the duct tape, the rage of the brainless in his eyes. So much for a conversation about the meaning of prophecies from the time before.

I have to feed him, but that is a problem. I take off the duct tape, he screeches, and now it's the Alamo in Northeast Philly. He starves to death, I accomplish nothing. Well, he can go hungry today.

I get atop one of the prison towers, and look West across Pennypack. It's evening, and the sun sets trailing the sky with pink ribbons like a ten year old girl's birthday party. I open a coolish Bud, my once-a-day, and toast myself, the last guy in animal control.

18. Animal Traps Are Safe?

As I'm up there, I thought about the events of the day. The odds aren't right.

Okay. You're saying, TC, you said it was a suicide mission. You said you were trying to save humanity because of that terrible shit you did. Remember? You hid while your AFE family was eaten alive. Of course the odds aren't right. You don't deserve good odds. You suck.

Thanks for saying all that, as if it wasn't all I ever thought. You're right. I deserve to die and that's why I took it all on. But I took it on 'cause I thought maybe it'd work out and I'd save the world. I mean, I'm giving myself one in a thousand odds, but . . . this live-catch-and-not-release program is not going to work out. They're always in packs. If that female had a sharper nose, I'd be running naked, wiping snot into my pubes, my mouth full of viral blood.

I don't want to catch them by hand anymore. Traps are clearly the answer. I go to sleep thinking about traps. I dream of traps. Pits and nooses and closing doors.

In the morning I go down the hall to the cell. Foxy stares at me, chewing on his duct tape. I've been so busy thinking how to get him roommates, I forgot I needed to feed the one I already had. It comes to me then. I go to the room where I've got a store of food and make up some oatmeal. I come back and open the cell door. He sort of butt hops at me but I put a knee into his chest and gently push him into the ground, with my weight on top.

Part of this is to treat them human all the time. That might help them remember. I've got a syringe, the type for giving babies medicine. I poke a small hole in the duct tape and insert the syringe. I squirt oatmeal in there.

"Here you, go, big guy. Just a couple days and you'll pull out of it." I hope. He eats the oatmeal, and then I pull him somewhat upright. His eyes have the same wolf-expression, animal anger. "I'm your buddy. I brought you shorts." This doesn't seem to change his mind about me, but he looks a lot more human in the shorts. "Be good and I'll get you a shirt."

The problem with a trap is, the second they realize they are caught they screech and their buddies would claw, scratch and bite them out. Even if they didn't get them out, they'd be there surrounding the entrapped VB- so how would I get them and take them to my rehab, without getting bit? The other problem would be suicide.

Raccoons caught in a trap chew their leg off to get free. Usually they bleed to death. VBs work the same way, like when Foxy head-butted the foot thick concrete wall of this Holmesburg prison cell. He was trying to get out. He'd destroy himself if I didn't have him chained to the floor. The chain is locked to his cuffs so he doesn't choke himself.

So- I need to trap them, keep them from killing themselves, and keep the others from getting them out, and killing me when I show up. A hidden trapdoor won't work, because they'll screech if they can't be seen.

I explain these things to Foxy. It's nice to talk to someone, even if his brain is broken, and then part of me thinks that maybe hearing me talk will remind him how to talk. He lurches against the chains, strains against duct tape.

"Relax," I say. "I'll figure it out."

19. Swinging Blood Mouths

In the end I decide on the classic noose on the ground. I'll use a thin metal cable, so the VB can't gnaw through. I trap a pigeon in a cage.

I'm good at this; I've been doing it for a while. Angie taught me. Get a crate, some crumbs, a stick and a rope. Tie the string to the stick, prop the crate up with the stick, put the crumbs under the propped up crate. Wait until the pigeon is under the crate. Pull the string. Reach in, break the neck, and you've got dinner. If you wait until after dark, the VBs don's see the smoke. Put it in there with the feathers still on, and later the skin and feathers peel off in one crispy piece. Enjoy your small chicken.

Of course, the VBs prefer their meat raw so this pigeon stays in the crate, neck intact. I put him under a telephone pole. I use a rock tied to string to get my wire cable over the top arm of the telephone pole. I leave enough length so that the noose just lies flat. A little tension and the whole thing pops up off the ground and will cinch around the hungriest VB.

I take the other end and trail it along the ground, and get in a house. I'm not the fatty I once was so I need to make some kind of spring to get quick force that will close the noose and lift the VB off the ground. I find a step ladder, take this out on a half roof in the back of the house and use it to climb onto the main roof. I take five milk crates up there. These I fill with everything heavy in the house, weights, jewelry, nails, plates. I stack them together on the front edge of the roof, so I can watch the noose. I wire them together and lash the cable that runs to the noose to the whole thing. "Nice trap," I tell myself. I have to encourage myself. No-one else does.

I place a bow and arrow on the roof, along with about one hundred arrows. Hopefully it's a small pack. Then I sit and wait. While I was building the trap I felt good. I only thought about getting it done. Now, while I wait, I try to picture Angie's face, her high cheek bones, her black eyes, but it doesn't come up. Then I think that maybe that's some sort of justice, her face abandoning me like I abandoned her. Then I don't want to think anymore so I walk around the roof, hoping to see some VBs, but there is nothing.

It's a couple of hours when I spot a pack. It's small, about fifteen. One of them smells the pigeon, or something like that. They swivel almost as one, and a faster one, a female is out in front. Her breasts bounce like dog ears. When they see the crate with the pigeon in it, they screech. She reaches it first, leaping on the cage.

At that moment I shove the weight off the house. Zip. The cable sings as the weight pulls it across the brick. The noose cinches around her torso and one arm, and jerks her up. She bobs, fifteen feet off the ground. The pigeon cage falls through the air, smashing on the ground.

Her pack, not caring, or not noticing her flying up, falls on the disoriented pigeon, while she screeches from the air. In moments the bird is eaten, and they look up at her. A more nimble one, a boy, scales the pole, and grabs her, attempting to pull her down. This puts her in more pain, adding to the tension on the cable, and she screams, clawing at him, knocking him from the pole.

Kwanesha taught me archery along with her advice about not being a bitch ass. You could kind of say her lessons had two elements: how to do real shit, and how to think about shit. Really, they went together. You had to be able to do real shit to think about shit like you could boss it. All that to say, I feel good, like I'm about to handle some shit, when I pick up the bow.

I slot an arrow onto the string and aim. I pick the biggest one, a hairy male. Arrow through the chest. He grunts. They looked surprised for about ten seconds, glance around, and see nothing. Then they start to eat him. Meanwhile the one I caught is still screaming. I know I couldn't enjoy a meal, no matter how good, with a dirty naked person screaming above me.

When the second arrow hits the crowd they start staring around. I watch, waiting, but after a long ass minute they still don't go back to eating. I'm low, behind a chimney on the roof, notching another. I shoot again. One of them sees where the arrow came from and is screeching and running toward the house. I got another arrow for her. They all figure it out now though, and the remaining ten or so are charging toward the house. I take two before they reach the front door.

Then I hear them, up the stairs like a herd of elephant-people, clawing at the ceiling, before one of them finds the window to the half roof. He puts his hand out, and I grab him, yanking him out and hurling him off. SCREECH-crunch. The others are in a knot, all trying to get out the window at once. I load up the bow and shoot an arrow in there. Screeching, snarling. I shoot another. Then one is coming out. I slip up a step ladder onto the main roof, and give it a good kick. The thing flies off the roof, and they are piling out onto the half. I've got Ackee out. "Com'on, freaks," I say. One is polite and does just what I ask, leaping and grabbing the main roof. I slam Ackee in the back of his head, but while I'm doing so two more are scrambling up. I sprint back the length of the roof. The other two are up and then there are four of them and I've got nothing but Ackee.

Bad odds. Using a rag to protect my hand I go down the plate and jewelry crate weighted cable like a fireman. One leaps after me, but the crack sound lets me know he broke his leg. The others are sliding, but they don't have a rag to protect their hands, and let go higher than me. The first lands in a tumble and I get a good Ackee slam on him before the other two are up. I'm thinking, "This shit is cray."

I'm pretty out of breath so I hold Ackee in front of me and back away. Two. Not bad. Two I can do, if I can just catch my breath. Then I sort of trip, and they snarl, and prepare to dart forward, but I've got my feet under me. The thing I tripped over was a brick. Nice. I reach down, making threatening motions every so often. Then I have the brick. I hurl it at the one, and bring Ackee down on the other. I hit the face and don't kill it as much as blind and mangle it. Different kinds of fluid start out of the punctured face. The other VB has recovered from the brick shot, but one on one is no problem. Ackee slam, twist and dead.

I go back and make sure all of them are dead. One I caught with an arrow in the mangle getting out the window is doing okay, and I have to knife it. I get back the arrows I can, wiping them down carefully, and then I wipe down Ackee. Then I get the cable and cut it, holding onto the end, and lower my newest pet slowly.

"What do you think, Dusty?" The name fits 'cause she dirty all over, and cause her hair is a dust colored matt. "I kicked some ass, huh?" She didn't seem impressed. I duct tape her, strap her onto a running stroller and start jogging for Holmesburg.

"Foxy is waiting for you. He says my conversation is too smart for him, but you are probably just his type. His type of talker, I mean."

20. Good Trap, Bad Trap

I end up setting up Dusty at the opposite end of the hall from Foxy. I think that VBs being with one another just encourages them in their viral beastliness. If they are alone the odds are better they'll pull out. I get her locked up, and squirt some oatmeal into her. I've decided to feed them no meat, since that seems to be all they ate before they joined me here. Maybe the veggies will take the hunger for flesh out of them.

I examine her. Okay with the jokes. Honestly, looking at her shape, she'd have been attractive, she somehow still had some plump to her curves, but the wild look in her eyes, it didn't seem like she was human. Nothing there, so shut up. She had a couple broken ribs. The arm that was in the noose wasn't broken, just badly bruised, but she'd need time to heal. "Sorry, Dusty. Sometimes salvation feels like you're being yanked off the ground by a metal wire." She didn't laugh. My jokes suck.

On the side of her cell someone had scrawled, *I need a woman.* It was like he is here in ghost form, speaking to me, asking for me to bring him a companion, just like Adam asked God about getting a woman.

"Hey," I say to the ghost of the inmate, "this is not a woman. But we're working on it."

After I feed my guests, I head back for the tower. There I once again sip on a once-a-day and think about what happened that day. It had all gone a little cray.

Mostly at first I'm just like, "Fuck yeah, I kicked some VB ass today. I killed twelve of those motherfuckers." I feel pretty gangster but then at some point it wears off.

The thing is, the fight I fought today, where I risked everything, where I went crazy, where the adrenaline kicked so high that I was buzzing, shaking as I killed the last one, that should have been seven months ago for my family. With my family. That was why I took the risk today, because I wanted to do something to save humanity, because I owed three humans.

So that brings me back to my commitment to success. I mean, I believe I will fail and this is a suicide mission, but the odds of me doing what I did today again, for even a couple more times, and surviving, are basically zero.

I have to think of a better trap.

21. Better Trap?

The problem is that VBs come in groups. The smallest packs are over ten, and the average is probably fifty. Fighting packs is a no go plan. I can't use firearms on them because it makes too much noise, any VB within miles will be running toward me. Using bow and arrow and Ackee is just too risky.

For the next couple of days I feed Foxy and Dusty and tell them stories. I put clothes on them which actually makes Dusty look a lot more attractive. I figure she looks more like an actual person with a tee-shirt and a pair of sweats on, but I know she isn't really. Foxy follows me with angry eyes and tries to spit out his baby food. "You angry 'cause I got a girlfriend? Don't worry, Foxy. You're still my number one."

The worst part of this is their shit. At first their shit came out dark and smelled like death- that's what happens when your diet is raw rat and squirrel with a slow pigeon thrown in now and then. Now it's a lighter color, and while it's still not my favorite odor, but I can kind of deal with it. They manage not just to shit, but to roll in it. I can change the clothes, and just throw the others out, I'm in a city full of clothes, but they get it in their hair too. I'm washing out Dusty's hair, which I've cut pretty close, 'cause it's not the first time this happened. She doesn't appreciate the cleanup and is struggling around.

"What? You want shit in your hair?" She might be nodding. Suddenly she twists and starts up, throwing me off, and then she's up.

She's headed for the cell door, the long chain trailing from her cuffs ringing like Christmas bells on the concrete floor. I must have forgot to lock it to the metal hoop. The smell of shit can seriously fuck with your concentration.

I walk after her. She glances wildly in each cell she passes, but I've secured them all, cinder-blocking up the holes created by saplings. She reaches the end of the hall, and swivels. She comes back toward me, her walk like a stomp, limp and run balled into one- her arms are locked behind her back, and that makes her awkward. She comes straight at me, which is less scary with her mouth duct taped, but then it looks like she wants to ram me to death, so I sidestep her, let her go past three big steps, and I stomp down on the chain. Her arms jerk out behind her, and then she falls hard on her ass. I drag her back to her cell and throw her in. "You're a shithead," I say. Her skull is smeared with stink brown. She just glares. "I'm the world police force, shithead. You better do what I say."

That's when I figure it out. The trap that works. It takes a couple days of wandering to get everything I need, but then I'm set. The next day, at Rhawn and the Boulevard, in the middle of twelve lanes, a jogging pack of fifty sees three rats in a cage. They run for it. They don't think too much about the context. To them, it's rats in a cage, surrounded by a white metal box. If they knew how to pray they'd thank God for his generosity. As the first two leap into the door, the doors slam behind them. The two inside ignore this, intent on breaking open the rat cage.

It's the blood mouths on the outside of the white metal box who are upset. They punch at the metal. They want rat too. But then the metal white box starts moving, faster and faster, and then they can't keep up with it, and they see a blue and yellow stripe under the word "Police".

22. Good Cop

Well, not really. I'm no good. But these blood mouths are definitely under arrest. I had drilled a couple holes in the roof of the paddy wagon, bolted some eye-holes in the holes, and run some cables through the eyes that were attached to the back doors. The second I saw I had two in there, I pulled the cord, the doors slammed shut, and I drove.

This is only the beginning of the process. I have to get them tied up. I drive them out to the Northeast airport. I need some space for the next step. It's a nice drive. No radio, and two crazy people growling behind me, staring at my ears. Whenever we pass a pack of naked people they chase us. Even when we're almost out of sight, I can see them in the rearview; they are still running after us.

I drive into a wide field of the airport. I figure if any packs are close on me I'll have plenty of time to get back in the wagon here. I leave the engine running, and go around. There is a lot of banging going on inside. I open the backdoor. Behind that there is a grate. The grate has a square hole in it, big enough for feeding prisoners. The biggest prisoner reaches through this, trying to grab me. He's got a lot of beard and hair, all pretty dark. I call him Harry.

Hey, Harry," I say. I give him a handshake, holding the hand in place, and while his wrist is there, I handcuff it. I twist the arm down, and lock the cuffs to the grate. Then I open the grate. The other one, not locked to the paddy wagon, comes charging out. When he's about four feet away, I sidestep, dropping a loop of wire cable over his head as he goes by. I cinch it, and drag him in, he's chomping and clawing but a little tap on the head from a baseball bat ends all that. "I'll name you Speedy," I tell him. He looks disappointed, like he was holding out for Smarty. Then I give him the cuff and the duct tape outfit all the AFE Holmesburg inmates are wearing.

The guy in the van isn't as hard, because he can't move, with his one arm locked up. Then I take them back. This is the terrifying part. Cars are dangerous. VBs will follow a car for miles, and while they can't keep up, if they are within a mile of you when you stop, they're going to find you.

Once you stop, you could be stopped two minutes, and out of nowhere one hundred blood mouths are sprinting at you. I had a plan this time though. I'd found a garage. It was about three city blocks from Holmesburg, and the door was not that loud and manually operated. I drove in garage which I'd left open, hopped out and slid the door down. I went upstairs, where I'd stowed some weapons, but the main plan was to wait fifteen minutes, and hope no packs showed up. When they didn't we'd walk over to the prison.

It worked fine. One pack ran through about five minutes later, but they saw no sign of us and kept moving. I dragged the two up to the prison. There I introduced them to Foxy and Dusty. They all acted real excited to see one other. I talked to them about shitting in the pails I had provided but they all just looked at me like I was the biggest idiot in the world. "Hey, at least I talk." I thought about hitting them in the head with the baseball bat but I wasn't sure if that would help them out of it. If they were

75

ever going to shake out of it. I used to see some kind of thinking in their eyes but after cleaning up a thousand shits I am thinking I made that up.

It doesn't really matter though. I've got nothing else to do with my days, so this is what I do. The paddy-wagon trap works. Sometimes it fails, if there is a VB in the van doors as I pull the cord, it bounces against them, and doesn't lock. At this point I start driving anyway. The ones in the paddy wagon jump out, and I have to try again. But when it fails, I'm still alive.

The percentages I can justify and I keep using it. I tend to get really fast VBs which isn't ideal if they ever get a chance to escape. The bigger ones I give a couple pairs of ankle cuffs I found.

When I have about fifteen duct taped VBs in there, I decide I'm at capacity. Obviously Holmesburg could fit a lot more, but the problem for me is that I've got to clean their shit and feed them on the daily. I do work out a thing where duct tape and a tee-shirt become a diaper, and their face masks get a little nicer as I get experience. I have to check them constantly. If once they get a mask off and start screaming, that's the end of me.

So that's my day. I don't get to forage for comics anymore. It's all food, tee-shirts to use as diapers, and duct tape reinforcements. I'm stockpiling guns too. Part of me believes that guns will come in at the end, though using them is always the last resort.

In the tower, I looked out over Pennypack, the snaking curves of the creek catching the last of the sunlight, reflecting through the trees. I ran across a bottle of red wine in a house, and that is my once-a-day. It says something in French or some shit on the bottle, and I'm a little weird about it, but when I taste it, it's like so much is going on with that flavor. It's like up and down and tingles into the corners. I'm wondering why this is the first time I'm drinking it.

It's good enough that I forget about the smell of shit for a while. I forget about the fact that my life is interacting with weird and broken non-humans in the impossible hope that they'll turn back human.

23. I'm a Mom

I got to be honest. This sucks. You probably never experienced a situation where every time you smelled your fingers no matter how long you washed, you smelled shit, but that is my life. Not only am I collecting it, I'm going out of the prison, carrying it in sacks and dumping it. The smell is too strong and if I kept it in here VBs would nose us out. As it is, they find the places where I dump it. I don't want to talk about what happens then. Just remember that VBs are basically human dogs but with less self-respect.

That's a couple hours, twice a day, diaper changes, wipe downs. Some of them will relax and let me wipe the smears from their legs and whatever they got between them, but a lot start struggling and I've got to tie them up. Then feeding them. I do this after I take a break when I finish the first clean off. They all are getting thinner, and none of them came in here fat, but I try to get food in them. I've got a lot of juice I been using, concentrate is best. The more calories the better. Not Gatorade, I'm talking Kool-Aid. I also pulled Hugs out of corner stores whenever I could. Turns out that hugs don't go bad. That neon food dye is like an anti-biotic. A hug, in case you aren't from Philly, is a small Kool-Aid style drink, neon blue, orange, red, or lime colored, that tastes like sugar. They used to cost almost nothing, now they cost nothing. Baby food, oatmeal, grits. Anything I can put in them without taking off their mask.

Along the way I read the walls of the prison cells. Crazy Bob still has the best wall. "All is fucked! Yet Pennypack will wash the Northeast carrying away their televisions and their sports gear. The Wissahickon shall surge, and its mighty torrent shall be like a herd of horses trampling through Chestnut Hill's self-assurance, and the widely placid Delaware will turn turbid, boil up and flood the Jersey woodlands, wash the Kensington streets of needles, Bridesburg shall shed its racism. Tiny Tacony shall transcend into a river through Olney." Weird dude. Would have been a poet if he wasn't a criminal. "What do you think, Foxy?"

Of course the most important thing is to try and civilize them. I remember my first grade teacher dealing with us. We weren't that different from VBs, still capable of shitting our drawers, snot faced, not knowing what to eat, unable to color in the lines, and she could loll us into a nap-like-quiet by reading books. She would circle us up and read "Matilda", emphasizing the words like they mattered, like we mattered, and we calmed, curled into cat-balls on the floor, and listened.

I read to them. At first I try comics, but comics are really in the pictures, and I can't walk to fifteen cells and show them the pictures while reading. Also, there is a lot of violence in the comics, and I start to think that's not the thing. I end up going for the books our first grade teacher read. "Charlie and Chocolate Factory". At first I pretend like they are listening, but they aren't. They don't struggle more or less when I read. I keep doing it though. It may be for me, the illusion that we are like my first grade class, back before school turned into an insult filled hate show, where every kid did what they could to get to the top, and I was always a stepping stone.

Not that I'm bitter. Was I special? Was I any good? When some people actually gave a shit about me, did I repay them with love? So stop crying. If there is a God he got his cards mixed up and let a piece of shit be the last man.

But all this work reminded me of my mom. As I holed up in my room through the teenage years, she came to the door again and again. "I made you hot dogs, T." "You want ice-tea?" "You okay, darling?" "I just got a call from the school, T. Turn off the game, we need to talk." I never noticed it. How much she did, I never noticed it. It was always there, like air to breathe. I didn't notice the thousand ways she carried my shit. My sadness. My fear. My hunger.

So I clean their shit, feed them, and read to them. I wish I knew some science, some shots or medicine I could try, and then I think, "What the fuck." These things are disposable anyway. I pick Harry. He is my least favorite because he always struggles when I'm wiping shit off his balls. I try to tell him that if he relaxes he'll find it's not bad, but he doesn't listen.

I start with aspirin. I move on to anti-biotics. I decide against steroids for obvious reasons. I give him an old flu-shot. Nothing. I make a mental note to stop in a pharmacy. I look at my inmates. "We need a doctor," I say. They look at me chewing on their duct tape. "Probably one of you knew some science," I say. Nothing. Idiots.

I go to the tower. I do not want to drink. I contemplate suicide. This life is terrible. The pleasure of one glass of wine at the end of the day is nothing compared to the pain and disgust of a day being these things mom. I don't think they are going to change. It's been two years. Any of them that were going to change back already did, already got killed. This is what's left.

The only reason I don't is because that's running away from it all, and the last time I ran away from it all, I left the three people that mattered most.

I live, Jim, because you fought for your family when there was no fucking hope. I heard you weeping when Kwanesha turned.

I live, Kwanesha, 'cause you'd have called me a pussy for even thinking about killing myself. You knew life was shit, and we fight through it for the clean moments in the shower.

I live, Angie, 'cause I owe you too much, and it hurts so much to be alive, and that hurt is the only way I know to pay down the debt. Oh shit, I miss you.

24. Forager

I tried to find comfort from the loneliness by foraging. It always made me think as I walked through a house from before. You see the family photo, the hockey gloves, the skates. The golf clubs. Dirty underwear. Sexy underwear. Bank statements. A picture would develop of a family that played hockey, paid the bills most of the time. Drank a lot. And I'd think what it might be like to be part of that family. I'd imagine I was their son.

It had gotten harder to take that portal into the lives of yesterday. A couple of things had happened. First, most houses had started to break down a little. At this point it wasn't the roofs; it was the animals. Animals like opossums and raccoons and rodents had multiplied like crazy 'cause there was whole supermarkets full of food for them to eat. A few got caught by the VBs, but you have to imagine it's like only five percent of the people that used to be here, and those people chase animals but they don't use guns or even sticks, just teeth.

Good thing most of the raccoons escape. I wouldn't want to see a raccoon VB. The animals had gnawed holes in the houses, and lots of windows were busted, so moisture got into the house, and the animals shredded beds and couches, making nests.

When I go into a house now it's not perfectly preserved snapshot of the family. It's there, but it's under a pile of shreds, shit and rodent smells.

I paused in a girl's room. She must have been fourteen or fifteen. Her walls are pink, with flowers and hearts stenciled around the borders. The bed has a pink blanket and some kind of opossum nest it. I kick the bed and the thing hisses at me, eyes bulging, showing needle sharp teeth. I unstrap Ackee and kill it. I don't allow animals to hiss at me. I'm the last fucking man. Plus, dumbass opossum, you're supposed to play dead.

Then I feel kind of bad. The opossum was sane, like me. But HE HISSED AT ME! Well, no use crying over dead opossum. I bag him up. I won't feed him to the inmates, but I'm not adverse to a little bit of meat now and then. That should give his death some meaning, some dignity.

The girl had posters of Katy Perry on her wall. Katy Perry sang all those songs about being you and living your dreams. Ha ha. This future was only in people's nightmares. Maybe you could say that in this future the people really are themselves. I think that a lot, but I'm real negative about people, including myself.

Pink-room girl had some stuffed animals. Most of them must have pissed off the opossum the same way he pissed me off, because they were tatters. Then I find a diary in a bedside table drawer. Inside it says, "Property of Alicia Huron. Don't read. MOM!"

I flip to the last couple entries.

August 15, 2014
I think Dan likes me. He asked me what I was doing after school and I was like, nothing but then he said we should hang and I remembered I had violin lessons so I said hey

i'm sorry I totally forgot that i have lessons. He totally looked really sad and then I was like, what about tomorrow and then he looked happy again so we said we could meet at the park and walk. I can't wait!

She dotted her 'i's with hearts.

August 16, 2014
I went to the park, but Dan wasn't there. I was walking and all the sudden these crazy ppl ran through the park, I swear they had blood on their mouths and someone was running from them. I hid in some bushes and then i ran home and saw some more ppl like that, and I was like is this some weird prank, you know like a flash mob of fake vampires? But I told mom and she said call the police and I said no it's weird so she called the police and just waited. I'm like whasup and mom said no one was answering. But I totally forgot that Dan didn't show up and I was sure he liked me from when he was smiling and when he wasn't.

That was the last entry. You and I can guess how it went from there. I'm no lover of pink, but I wanted to live in a world where girls who had pink bedrooms could worry about whether or not Dans like them. Now Alicia Huron was an animal who'd like to gnaw on me. I grab some tee-shirts out of her bureau and stuff them in a trash bag. Diapers for the babies.

It made me wonder what Angie's room looked like before AFE. I figure it didn't look like this. She probably had a simple color on the walls. White or something. She wouldn't have painted it. Probably have posters up. And no Katy Perry. Her music had an edge to it, Drop Kick Murphys. Lil Wayne. Still, I thought it would have felt like this, small and carefully arranged and neat. Like a nest on a slender branch, separate from anything dangerous, safe. A place where a girl growing up could keep a diary. Write about a first crush.

I hear screeching. A great big pack, like over a hundred of them, is running down the block. I duck back from the window and the front runners go by, and I peek again. It's weird, I see the one that I thought was Angie again. It's too risky to look again. I'm waiting for them to go by, when a screeching that is louder and continuous starts up. This is bad. I venture a peek and a female is facing the house I'm in, screeching, looking at the house, and the others turn, and start in.

I run out in the hall. I hear them ransacking the living room. They're looking for me; she must have smelled me.

Fuck. I hurl the opossum down the stairs. I figure the opossum'll distract them for a second. I have a bow with me and Ackee. No gun. I can't kill one hundred. I can try to defend the stairs, but they'll get in the second story windows eventually. I can try to run out a window, but a glance shows that won't work. They're surrounding the house, and they'll see me. I run, on my toes, to the back of the house. Snarling and then the snapping of the opossum's tendons sounds from the crowd at the bottom of the stairs. I glance out the window as I hear them charging up the stairs. There are VBs on the ground. I grab the roof gutter and pull myself up on the roof. I think maybe I'm making it until the VBs on the ground let up an insane screeching. They must have seen my dangling feet. I get upright on the slanty roof and turn.

"Thanks," I say to the screechers. I give them the finger so they can know it's sarcastic. They keep screeching. Then human fingers are on the gutter, where mine had just been. I wait until I see her face, a bitch haloed by clumpy hair, and slap her with the pointy end of Ackee. Down she goes, done with screeching. It does nothing to quiet the place 'cause they are all the rest of them going full power. Okay. I do a couple more. Like that game in arcades where you hammer the moles when they pop up. I could do this all day, but they will be coming up other ways soon. Still, I risk head shotting about five more. The ground VBs are pretty occupied with eating their dead. Then it's too dangerous to stay here with my back toward any others that might get on the roof from a different window. I climb up to the peak, and string an arrow.

I'm not going out without a fight. They come up from one window and another. I shoot one and then the next. Then it's three up there at once, charging from different sides. No time to string an arrow. I run along the ridge of the roof to meet the first one and get rid of him, but the other two arrive simultaneously. I'm at the high point, with them both crouched below on opposite sides. One leaps, grabbing my shoulders, forcing me down to my knees. His teeth chomp the air, his blood-spit sprays all over my face (I close my mouth and eyes). I hold him back but can't push him away, he's too strong. His teeth inch toward my face. I drop to the roof, rolling him on top of me, and then kick, so he spins, losing his grip, over me. I release him and he bowls into the other one, and they roll in a ball down off the roof. Screeches double as they go down, and the sounds of flesh ripping follow shortly after. "You guys are disgusting," I yell.

At that point I'm able to use the bow and arrow. I spit seven more with arrows. They fall, grab at the roof, and when they've lost enough blood, they let go and roll off. I've only got a few arrows left. Anyway they are getting up here too fast, and I quickly shoulder the bow and unhook Ackee. TC's last stand. The final go. Come on, bitches. Let's do this.

It's ten or eight, or twelve. I don't know. I stop being able to do things like math. They are advancing, a tightening ring, like lions I saw in this documentary once that surrounded an elephant. They all jumped on it at once, biting, until its back boiled with lions. They leap. I hit, dodge. One grabs back. I hold his wrist and pull and he goes flying over. Before I can unbend another tackles me and we are rolling across the roof. He is chomping at my trousers.

He leans away, my canvas pants rend and he plunges down to find the flesh past the fabric. I grab his hair, and stop him for a second, but his neck muscles are stronger than my arm. He moves toward my leg, and I can see the virus bearing blood running on his teeth. With my other hand I flick a knife blade through his throat. The blood releases along with his hands, and he rolls off. A roar from the crowd below. I turn to the others, who are scrambling after us.

Ackee-less, but it doesn't matter. The hate for this time and this way of being rides my blood like super powers, and I'm moving faster than I thought I could. I dart at the nearest one, catch him by his dick and yank. He plummets, yowling. Another leaps and I duck and jump, knee into his mid-section, and he rolls over the edge.

Then I grab Ackee, and face the last six. It's as if time has stopped. They roar and raise arms, but I slip through their grasping fingernails, past their chomping canines, and deliver, one after another, death blows. The last one I'm really hammering on the skull, just smearing the brain across the roof, when I realize I've kind of lost it.

I retrieve the bow, and take my position on the roof peak, with an arrow on the string. I wait for the next wave. I keep waiting. Nothing is happening. In fact there is no screeching. I know there was more in the street than I killed, though I've got no idea how many I killed. I walk down to the edge of the roof and look. I see them down on the ground. They are lying down in the shade, piled on top of one another. I look down straight and see the almost stripped skeletons of the newly dead. All the flesh has been gnawed off them. The living have eaten their fill, and are digesting.

It's over.

I look among the piles for the one that looked like Angie. They are so lumped together I can't pick her out, and I might have killed her anyway. It's possible, of course, that she's out here somewhere, but the odds of me finding her suck pretty hard.

I get down. I'm careful; I've got an arrow to the string, but I am able to get back in the house and walk down the stairs, and out the front door without any confrontation. One or two look up from their human piles and growl at me, but they can't move. I want to kill them all but I'm exhausted so I jog off.

25. Maybe it was her

I actually puke on the jog home. The idea of them just eating one another to the point where they were in a fall-down food comma. It was a little weird though, because that wasn't anything new to me. I'm asking myself what is the big deal, and then I remember I saw one that looked like Angie. The idea of Angie doing that, gorging on raw human, is what makes me sick. And she probably is, somewhere.

The one I saw, the look-a-like was the same one I'd seen a few weeks ago. I thought it wasn't her because of the jaw line, but now I wonder what hunger and a diet of rats, and let's face it, humans, would do to her jawline. I thought of course I'm thinking this because I would imagine any female with dark hair and her build was her. But I had to realize, I wouldn't know for sure unless I took a close look. That was going to be dangerous but what the fuck. All I felt was guilt for the last time I hadn't tried to save her, if I didn't make sure this time I'd just add to it.

A decision. Go back to Holmesburg and tend to the inmates, or go back to the house where I slaughtered them, and see if Angie is there.

Then I think, they are going to just lie there and sleep for at least twelve hours. They aren't going anywhere, gorged on human meat. Anyway, if I decide it is Angie, or close enough, I better have weapons, 'cause I'm going to get her, or die trying. Fine. I start jogging again, and soon I'm back at Holmesburg.

I'm moving quick through the cells. The VB babies don't get ass wipe downs this time. They just get a diaper change and a couple squirts of oatmeal. "I've got a date," I tell them, and they nod and wish me luck. Then I reach Dusty's cell, and she's looking at me, not struggling against her chain.

Her eyes look pretty intelligent. She's looking at me like she's trying to figure it out (not like I'm lunch). I've been waiting for this moment but it couldn't be timed worse.

"Blink if you understand English," I say.

She blinks. "Oh shit," I say. "Pardon my language," I add. She is looking at me, her eyes starting out of her head. Then she backs away from me to the end of the chain. Far side of the cell. At first I'm like, "Why are you backing away from me? I'm the only human around." Then I see it from her perspective. I do have a club and knives on my belt. She is chained up, duct taped and under my control, in a cell. She thinks I'm some weird serial killer.

26. Dilemma

Dusty is looking at me with terror in her eyes, backed up as far as the chains will let her get from me. Terror is a good sign of sanity, I've never seen it in a VB. For weeks I've been waiting for one of these crazy prisoners to show me a look with this much intelligence. Now that it's here, I don't want to deal with it. I want to go and find out if I saw Angie.

Okay. I can stay here for a minute. I say to my wide eyed prisoner, "Do you remember being a VB? Blink if you remember that." No blink. Great. "Okay. Listen. We're living at the end of the world. Some crazy virus came in and made people like animals. Whoever they bite turns to be like them, and as far as I know I'm the last person. I've been hiding from them, but then I decide to start catching them, and see if one pulls out. Remembers how to be human. That's you. You are the first crazy to be human again."

Her look is no less scared. It's a lot to process. Part of me is thinking that I should just leave her chained up, and go out with the paddy wagon and start mowing down the pack and separate out the maybe-Angie. Dusty's not going anywhere.

But then I think how scared Dusty is now. If I can just calm her down, she'll understand. She should be scared, but not that she's in a serial killer's basement. It's worse than that. Then I'll have a friend. If I leave her like this, go away and come back eighteen hours later, she might be crazy. Not VB crazy, but, waking up from a comma on a chain with duct tape over your mouth and staying like that for eighteen hours crazy. I've got to help her. That's the whole purpose of this project.

"But," I say, "This may be your only fucking chance to get Angie."

"Be logical," I say to myself. "It's not Angie. You just want it to be her that bad. Remember the plan. Stick to the fucking plan. It's the only way." Then I realize I've been talking out loud, a habit I have since it's nice to hear a voice, but it isn't going to help Dusty believe I'm a regular person.

"Fine," I think, "Dusty first."

I say, "I'm going to pull off the duct tape on your mouth. I have to tell you, you can't start screaming. I'll let you walk out of here. I will. But if you scream we die." She nods, but I don't trust it. It's the kind of nod that says, "Yeah, sure. Whatever you want. Whatever you say. You got knives, and some evil spikey club."

I say, "Look, I'm going to give you a tour with that thing on your mouth. After you've seen a little of what is going on, I'll take off the gag."

First I take her out of the room, and chain her to me with an extra set of handcuffs. "Sorry, you have to finish the tour before you leave, and watch me wash the last diapers." She sees the other VB inmates straining, bumping, wild-eyed. Of course it's behavior that you could imagine in any human chained up and duct taped silent. I can see that they aren't human, but how's she to know.

I take her up the tower. I give her the binoculars when I spot a pack. A small group, about fifteen, naked and blood mouthed. "Look. You see?"

She nods. "Okay. I'm taking off the duct-tape and handcuffs. Don't scream. We'll both die if you do." I rip the tape off.

She smiles when it comes off. She isn't shouting; that's good. Then I say, "Let me get the cuffs."

I'm anticipating a real conversation, an exchange of names, as I take off the cuffs. I unlock one wrist. I'm going for the other, when she rips them away. I look up and see the still cuffed wrist flash. A second later I'm down on the ground. She has slammed the cuffs into my head, which really hurts. Now she's booking down the stairs.

"Ah, fuck."

I get up. I better chase her. Idiot isn't going to get far. My head swings. Shit. I start down the stairs. Now I finally get one, and she gets eaten fifteen minutes later. I'm definitely not good at this.

I stumble down the stairs. She hasn't made it out this door, it's padlocked. But I find about two minutes later that she has made it out one I leave dead bolted for quick escapes. Finding an exit slowed her down, helped me catch up, and I see her as I get outside.

"Here I come, Dusty. Your nightmare." Not that I give myself a good chance of catching her.

27. Chasing Human (for a change)

I'm thinking at first that I won't be able to catch Dusty. She's only seventy yards in front of me, but she's a former VB. They are super fit from running non-stop, chasing deer, and people who are running super-fast. That is the speed people run, when they're running for their lives.

It's not that I don't run myself. When I'm foraging, I run between houses. When I'm not, I make sure to do a work-out of push-ups, sit-ups, and pull-ups that Kwanesha taught me. The idea is I want to be top form when I'm fighting the VBs. You can see how important that is.

But then I realize that even though she was VB, she's been chained in a room for over a month. The only workout she's gotten is straining against the chain and taking three steps. Maybe I'll catch her before the VBs do.

It's night. There is like half a moon, so you can see most stuff. Dusty is running fast away from me, not well either, I can hear the pitter patter of her feet. She also believes I was lying about the screaming killing us, because every so often she screams. They're going to hear her, and hunt her. I run silently, using the outsides of my feet, clinging to the shadows. I've got Ackee on me, but no bow.

She's going back by the house where Foxy used to live, you remember that place is a pack-den, the wood of the door brown and rounded by their passing. As she swings by them I see two pop out the window and take off after her. They shriek to wake up the rest. She turns and sees them. Two naked dudes with copper stained mouths running after her at a sprint. She screams and starts going faster. I guess me, as some lock-you-up-in-the-basement serial killer isn't as scary as VBs. Though I figure it's not like a comparison for her. She feels like she woke up in some nightmare shit, or maybe she's hoping this is a nightmare and she's still going to wake up.

She is charging down the footpath into Pennypack, the two VBs behind her, and then me last, but soon enough I'll be followed by these guys' buddies. It's darker in there, the trees shredding the moonlight. It falls across the asphalt ribbon in the shape of knives. I barely see her but I see them, and they are closing on her, and getting further from me. Like I say, you don't beat a blood-mouth in a distance race.

The two of them are screeching. Going to alert the pack. I have to do something. I yell, "Yo, blood mouths!"

They haven't heard a human yell in ages. They turn, more weirded out than anything. I unsling Ackee and enter the melee. They are bigger than average, and as I approach, they crouch, low to the ground. This is going to be difficult. I yell, "Come back and help, lady. You got me in this mess." She has stopped and is watching. I figure she's thinking back through her run, realizing that all the houses are shells, the streets are filled with vehicles parked in the middle of the street, and she hasn't seen a sane person yet. Beside me. And we know how she feels about me.

No, but if she can think she'll realize that everything I said is true and maybe she can trust me. Of course it's hard to think when you're out of breath and running for your life.

The VBs come toward me, breathing heavy. I threaten with the weapon. They fall back for a second, watching for a moment of weakness. I dance at one and he shrinks back, then at the other. In the dark they look the same. I don't have time for this. I figure the VBs know. They know their pack will come soon. Proving that idea one of them shrieks. I take a swing and he dodges. I do this a couple of times, circling one way. They aren't between me and Dusty anymore.

I take off running after Dusty, who is stopped half a block down the path, watching the fight. When I start running after her, she starts running too. The VBs are behind me, running again. It's kind of like when you play train as a kid and you switch who is going first, but there is one kid who is always in front. This is a recipe for death by the way. I never let them run me to ground. By the time they catch you, you are winded and can't fight and then you are eaten. I've seen it happen too many times.

I yell, "I need help. This is not the world you remember."

The VBs gain on me. In one motion I stop dead, drop to a knee, and turn, swinging Ackee. I catch the first one full in the face, two of the tines burying themselves in the old bloodstains. In a single movement I stand and wrench the weapon from his face, the tines turn, tearing flesh, and come loose.

His brother is not eager to engage. He stands back further than before, and lets out a horrendous shriek that seems to curl the tree leaves. He is answered by a bunch of shrieks, coming from the way we came.

I remark to myself, "This is terrible." Meanwhile the Pennypack, fat brown creek, runs silent and calm under the moon. I take off running again.

"Hey, my name is TC," I yell.

She yells back, "I'm Theresa." She is still running. I like Dusty better.

I say, "We're going to die if we run whatever random place you think of. If you let me lead, we've got a chance."

"You're crazy."

"Who's crazier, me or these guys?"

She doesn't answer, and I can't talk anymore because I'm too out of breath. He's behind me, but not closing the distance. He doesn't need to. The crowd of shriekers behind him are definitely getting closer. Not only that, I can hear shrieking behind that group, as the news spreads. Somehow they know the difference between shrieks about squirrels and humans, and the shriek about humans is the most exciting. It calls up VBs for quite a distance.

She isn't responding anymore, just running. I can only go this way another minute. They are going to converge on us.

28. So Many Blood-mouths

I'm about to turn off and head for the house where I've got the paddy wagon and a lot of weapons, and have a last stand like the Baptist Army, when she stops. I catch up with her pretty quick. "Here," I say, and hand her a knife. We've got to establish trust. "Let's kill this one."

She shrugs. She doesn't use the knife on me, and she turns with me. I swing at the VB behind us. He's the one whose shrieks are bringing the rest. He backs away. She circles him and stabs at him. He jumps back, but this is all I need. I land a shot on his thigh and he goes down. I use another knife on his throat.

She gasps; I say, "This is the end of the world, girl. Killing these things is the least terrible thing you're going to see. Follow me." I take off sideways through the small trees, feet to the leaves. She follows. We run for about fifty yards and then I make her stop. The shrieks fill the night around us. The main group comes up to where we killed him. They stop for a bit, and then continue the way the path goes but I know it won't be long before they circle back. The night air is littered with their cries. They come from every direction.

We move along slowly. I whisper to her, "We'll catch our breath. We're going to have to run at some point. I have a house about two blocks from the edge of the woods. In it is a car, a paddy wagon with gas and keys. Once we get in that, we should be fine. Don't let them bite you. That's when you change."

"What is going on," Theresa-Dusty says.

"People went crazy. Some kind of virus. They pass it with their bite, but often they just eat up whatever they bite. They are still smart, but they don't talk or use tools. Like it's the same species, but no civilization or logic. I don't know if anyone else is left. And it isn't looking so good for us."

I don't bother yelling at her for cracking my head with the cuffs and running. There's no point, and what she did was reasonable. Even if it wasn't, who am I to hold somebody for something like that? I'm no saint.

I tell her, "5609 Shale Elm Rd. Paddy wagon in the garage. There's an AK-47 in the driver's seat, if we get separated."

The screeching continued around us. The group on the Pennypack footpath have turned around and are investigating the spot where we killed the one. They will be back on our trail in a second. "Try to be quiet," I say, and take off through the leaves. In the moonlight I can pick rocks and bare earth to walk on, but she's not so good and the crackling sound of leaves erupts with each step. I tell her, "That's as quiet as you got, you better have speed." I leave off the picking and run as fast as I can without losing breath. I'll save the sprinting for when we clear the trees. The screeches behind us amplify; they hear us; they're coming.

"I'm scared," Theresa-Dusty says.

"Good," I say. "You should be." The shrieks behind us are directing the shrieks in front of us. On all sides the shrieks

100

grow closer. I can hear the woods around us crackle as other sprinters join in. When we hit the open space past the trees, they are going to be everywhere.

"Use the knives only when necessary. The main thing is to keep moving and stay close to me."

Then we pass the last few trees and see, like a shotgun blast in reverse slow motion, the trajectory of the sprinters, the humans with no language. Straight at us. From every angle.

I don't count them. Too many. I run at the one that is most directly in the line toward the paddy wagon house. When we are a yard apart I dive into his knees. He goes flying and I'm back up. T-Dusty is at my shoulder. There are at least fifty behind us, and there are more in front, coming out from between the houses, emerging from behind cars. Everybody is sprinting.

Four or five are coming in- next avalanche. I tell her, "Jump into them."

For someone who's been a VB for a while, she's really fucking ready to go at them. We leap together, we the o-line for ourselves, fuck a block, and we hit them with knives and Ackee flailing. I don't know whether they're dead, or just injured, or maybe we went by them without a scratch. "YEAH!" I yell. "Civilization is back, blood-mouths!" Because there are two of us.

A second before the next wave. We're on a street, weed-lawns, houses, and rust-cars surround me. Maybe I slow up to hit them just right. Or maybe one is that fast. I don't know. Somehow, my ankle is grabbed at that moment and I sprawl-somersault onto my face. Going down is bad news. I roll. A VB smacks the section of street I just left, another flies over me into him. I pop up, but another plows into me. We roll, his snarler is yapping slashing. I twist away. The flecks of red stain my shirt. He springs through the air toward me, arms extended. On my back I can't swing, but I place Ackee's butt on the ground so he lands on it.

I'm up, wrenching the weapon from his rib cage. Dodge this way. Dodge that. This reminds me of Kill-the-Man, a game we played in elementary school. Everyone tackled the kid with the football. If you didn't want to get tackled you threw the ball away. I sure wished I could drop something and get them to leave me alone. I don't see T-Dusty anywhere.

It seems that they are everywhere, just at me, a hand grips my ankle or shoulder. I can't go down again. I knock the hands from my shoulder, I step high to avoid their fingers going for my feet.

Here's something you should know. Even in this moment I wouldn't change the All Fucked Era for the past age. Back then, it was video games, pizza, and nobody cared about me 'cause I had acne, cause I was fat. Even though all I did was play games, tried to have fun all the time, nothing fucking mattered. And that was the same for everybody. You going to be a doctor or a trash collector, buy some shit made in China, live for your own pleasure? Like a whole world built around the concept of wacking off. Too easy. Too nothing.

I don't want to die, so fucking bad. But I feel so alive. I've felt alive ever since AFE began. And along the way, I found out that some people were okay. I would never change it out.

The thing I'd change, right now, was the way I hid when they came for Jim, Kwanesha, and Angie. I wasn't no better than a VB that day, following instincts, doing the first thing. If this is the end, I'm a say it one last time to whatever of you three remain, in the cosmos or heaven or hell, or just in my mind maybe, I'm sorry. You deserved better.

29. What happened to the Baptist Army

You may remember when I told you about the Baptist Army. Back a long time ago, two three months in to AFE, that's where I met Jim and Kwanesha. The Baptist Army were led by Pastor John, a man as large as a small giant, who preached that the VBs were God's judgment on us for sexual immorality. Kwanesha always would argue that economic oppression was a worse sin, just to fuck with him 'cause I don't think she really believed in sin anyway.

Anyway, the why of what caused it wasn't the main point. The main point was that God wanted us to kill all the VBs so we could make a new life. Anybody was allowed to join. Jim and Kwanesha took up with one another, and they weren't married, and nobody said anything. Pastor John tried to pray them married one time but Kwanesha said there was no point in that since it was the end of the world.

The only condition to staying in was you joined in the Baptist Army mission. You didn't have to believe in God, or morality, or God's judgment. You didn't have to get married, or stop smoking pot, though we did that on the roof, just out of respect. You had to believe in killing VBs. The mission was to kill them all. We used to believe that. We worked on it all day. Killing, killing and more killing. It was some of the hardest work I ever did. You were tense the whole time, and blood, kidney, and brain matter made for a different kind of dirty.

Anyway, back then it wasn't that bad. We rested, talked, and watched as Pastor John tried to convince all the women that they needed to be married, usually to him, so we could re-populate the earth. There was a Rican girl there I liked but she was three years older than me. She was a nurse, so she had a lot of respect around the Baptist Army, important job, but she was cool with everyone, not trying to give unnecessary orders to show she could. Her name was Arianna. It was nice to have a crush, even if I had no chance. The point was that I could look at her, and see she was hot and imagine what it felt like to be close to her. I didn't like a lot about the Baptist Army, but they were family.

Also, back then it wasn't that hard to kill the VBs. They were solitary. They didn't fight one another, but you didn't see the pack mindset. If there was an obvious target, they all went for it kind of together, but without someone to try and eat they traveled alone kind of aimless.

We left the Baptist Army. I was the one who said, "Let's go," but Jim and Kwanesha were ready. They wanted to focus on one another with whatever time was left.

The way I look at it is this. There are two movies about roaches. One is *Men in Black*, and there the roaches are humongous, and alien, and killing people right and left. A special agent manages to blow them away. The other is *Joe's Apartment*. In that movie, he's like, "I can't get rid of the roaches." So he works with them.

Those are the two schools of thought with the VBs. Fight it out, to the death, or live with the VBs. We all, Jim, Kwanesha and me, had decided that it was a *Joe's Apartment* kind of scenario. There were more and more VBs and you could kill all day, and you could have blood

105

get murky cause the first blood puddles were dried and caked and new blood got on and turned the old stuff into mud. And then there were more.

And when we left, the VBs had starting using the shrieks to communicate. One sees someone, and it shrieks, and that alerts others. The others shriek too, and the news spreads. That was the end for a lot of people. Cause the news kept spreading, anytime they spotted you you'd have to fight every single one in the area, or escape somehow.

Me, Jim and Kwanesha didn't live far from Baptist Army, and sometimes we heard the sounds of their battle. We were good neighbors. It didn't matter that we didn't agree on what to do about the VBs. None of us liked the blood mouths. It was like a country neighborhood back then. You didn't see the neighbors often, and when you did it was time for a real catch up. At least that's how I think country people do it.

We'd drop by in the evening, when they weren't busy working. Then one time we went and they were still fighting. There were a ton of VBs, a crowd ten deep pushing at their warehouse, surging through the door. We didn't hear any humans, but Jim said they were still there, just too tired to talk. The Army needed help. Kwanesha said, "That's on them."

Jim said, "We got to help."

Angie had joined us but she didn't know them. She shrugged. They looked at me. I said, "If we can help them and not get hurt, it's okay."

So the way they had it set up was they had a warehouse where they would funnel the VBs in one single house size door and they'd kill them inside. The problem was, with the shrieking, the blood mouths kept coming, and they weren't going in the door non-stop, some were circling the warehouse, so the Army couldn't leave out the back door.

Angie said, "They got to get out of there."

I said, "Distraction?"

Jim said, "We've got to use a vehicle."

Kwanesha said, "It's too risky." I already explained this, but in case your dumbass forgot, the thing with vehicles, back in those days was that the VBs would follow them, and whenever you stopped a mob was running up on you. It is a little easier now because there are a lot fewer VBs. "Jim-Baby, you ain't getting in a car."

I said, "I'll do it." Now, this was risky, and I just said I was about the *Joe's Apartment* way but I was also about impressing Angie. That was actually a more important than living right then. I had imagined scenarios where I'd die and she'd love my memory. That seemed like a good reason to die.

Kwanesha shrugged, which was an okay. Angie said, "Drive it slow around the warehouse until they are all following you. Honk a little. When you got the whole pack, drive North on the Boulevard a couple miles and then drive back down at full speed, we'll meet you in the Shoprite. Hopefully we can lose them with the store.

Kwanesha said, "He don't need no back up. If he get caught getting out of the car, what are we going to do?" This was a good point.

Angie said, "Yeah. Good luck."

I did it. It all worked. It was kind of fun, looking in the rearview and seeing a parade of animal humans chasing me. I felt important. Then I swung back around. When I got to Olney I left the car at a sprint and not a VB was there to see me. I met them back at the Baptist Army's pad. Everyone clapped, and Angie gave me a hug, and so did Arianna.

But after that Kwanesha tried to explain to Pastor John that they couldn't kill them all and that he was leading the Army to their deaths. Pastor John said it was the will of God that the blood mouths be destroyed. Kwanesha said if God gave a shit he'd never had let the All Fucked Era happen. Pastor John said God works in mysterious ways. Kwanesha said the VBs worked in strange ways, but everybody knew what the fuck they were and if anybody was so fucking ignorant to continue acting like you could fight them forever and win, they deserved to die. By now they were pretty much nose to nose. Jim kind of got between them. Kwanesha yelled for the rest of them to leave before it was too late, but none of them moved. They believed pretty hard. Heroes or idiots. Maybe it's the same thing. We waved them all goodbye.

The next time we went was a couple weeks later. Angie was getting bored looking at me. "Let's visit the Baptists," she said.

"Okay," I said. I always agreed with her, even though that time I was worried she wanted to meet guys. I started thinking about which single guys were in the Baptist Army. There were three young and healthy guys I was worried about.

We got Jim and Kwanesha to come along. When we got to the apartment it was empty so we went to the warehouse. The single door slapped open in the wind. We walked in. There they were. Some of them. Just bones. Not a lot of blood 'cause the VBs lap that all up.

Kwanesha said, "I told them."

Jim said, "Not now, baby."

I walked among them and wondered if Arianna was there. Pastor John was. You couldn't miss that big ass skeleton. In one of his boney hands he held his signature weapon, the baseball bat. The skull kind of looked like a grin, but it's hard to know. All skulls look like a grin. At least he died fighting.

That could be me. My bones and Ackee in the sun. Run, TC, run and live.

30. In the Shit

No moment was ever more hopeless for me personally. I mean, it was a worse moment when I hid when the VBs destroyed my family, but I was pretty confident I would make it out. On the roof, there might have been one hundred, but I had the high ground, a bow and that meant I got to fight most of them one at a time.

I'm running like crazy, juking right and left, and it's not doing any good. I get past one only to have three more converge. If it is my time I already said what I needed to say. I wondered briefly if Dusty would know what to do, how to run the prison, in my absence.

I saw a car. I jumped in and slammed the door. WHAM. A VB slammed against the window, his bloody mouth smearing the glass. Thank goodness it didn't break. I check for a key. No key. I wish I knew how to hot wire a car.

They bang with their heads and fists and heels against the car. They hit glass and metal. I place my hands and feet on the windows, trying to counteract the palm, heel and skull hits, but the passenger window cracks and then shatters. Hands and gnashing teeth surge, for a moment blocked by one another. I slam a foot down, pushing one head out, and follow it with Ackee. It sticks on something and I twist. A howl blossoms from the octopus of hands and mouths. Then a window on the driver side shatters. I slash with a knife at the hands that come grasping through it.

110

It crossed my mind that I should just give up. I was going to die. But then I thought that I had fought this far, and fuck if I couldn't take three or four more. I only wish I had a grenade like that Rican marine had in *Aliens*. Come on, motherfuckers, watch if I don't make this a long night.

I kind of imagine getting bit as a nice ass moment. I get bit and I don't have to think anymore. No memory of wrong. Just simple instinct. Everything as it comes. No future and no past just doing what I want. But I hate everything about it. I don't want to eat raw squirrel.

Then I hear honking, something I haven't heard in forever, and then headlights are beaming down the street! Straight at me! I barely manage to brace myself before BANG, a van plows into my car. The halfway-in VBs are thrown out, and a bunch are crushed. The van drives off about fifty yards and somebody leans out the window. I just make out the outline of the gun before I hear it.

TAT-TAT-TAT-TAT. You got to imagine. We live in a silent ass world. No semi trucks, no blasting systems, no house parties. That gun sounds like God barking. And those blood mouths fall like glass blowing under a strong wind, like in rows. They start chasing her. She shoots a couple more, and drives off. They follow her. I sit look around, and want to say thank you. I'm going to live. Then the paddy wagon is back, slowing down and then the passenger door pops open. I'm running, jumping, and I'm in.

"You saved my life!"

111

"YEAH," she yells.

She's holding the steering wheel with both hands leaning forward, her eyes bright. She is nodding. She runs down a couple more, "YEAH," she says and then offers me a high five. I give her five and she says, "YEAH!"

I tell her how to get back to Holmesburg. While she drives she says, "YEAH! YEAH! YEAH!"

31. Why Live With Guilt?

"So all you think about all the time is the one bad thing you did," Dusty says. She is a suburb girl, I forget which one, but you can hear her saying that I'm a dumbass in her way of saying it.

"Not all the time but it's the main thing."

Her voice gets a little softer. "I think you are being too hard on yourself, Tee. First off, I don't agree that you made a wrong decision. It might have felt sort of bad at the time, but you did was entirely logical. If you went up to help them, you would have just died too. Also, you can't live like that, trying to make up for your wrongs. When you make a mistake you don't feel all guilty and hate yourself. Everyone makes mistakes. You try to learn from them, you grow, but it's not the end of the world or anything. You can't pay for them. Who are you paying? Your old family is all dead.

I'd been wanting someone to say this stuff and now that I'm hearing it I get mad. Her arguments make a lot of sense in general but not to me. She didn't really understand that those particular people were better than me, and that me acting like my life had any value without them was fucking terrible.

I say, "You don't understand."

The second she rescued me in the paddy wagon, she was really excited. She was like, "Let's party! We made it."

113

I was like, "No, we got to drive by this house." I had her get close to the Pink-Bedroom House where I saw the maybe-Angie, and cut the engine. We were gliding in just as the sky was turning gray with first light. There was only one group left, the others must have headed for home. The group was just stirring, one of them up and murmuring, the others still piled close together. We watched. Dusty wanted to ask questions, but I didn't want them to notice us so I made her shut up. They got up, stretching, peeing, and then they grouped up, following the barking of one, and started to run along, their arms sort of floppy, red drool streaming off their mouths. Maybe-Angie wasn't with them, but I figured if we followed this group they'd take us back to the den, and she might be there. I told Dusty to follow them.

First we had the conversation where she apologized for hitting my with cuffs, running off, and almost getting us killed, but I told her it was no big, that kind of shit happens all the time here and it was nice to be attacked for a sane human reason every once in a while. Then we moved on to getting to know one another. She'd been a second year med student before this stuff hit. That was good news. I think she must have been cute because she kept checking her face in the mirror of the paddy, and trying to fix her hair. I guess she didn't appreciate my hair stylist skills.

She was surprised that I was only eighteen.

"Why," I said.

"I don't know, you look older." I realized that I'd grown up. I wasn't a pizza-ice-cream video-game-kid anymore.

114

After that she wanted me to explain the world we were in. I told her everything I knew about VBs and survival. She wanted to know if there were other people and I said I didn't know. People had to hide so it was hard, but I also noticed that the VBs seemed not to think there were people either. They hunted forests and sewers more than houses.

She thought the VBs were weird. She said, "How come I got my memory?" I didn't know. She said, "It's like part of the brain is turned off, but it's hard to know what. Wish I was a brain surgeon."

Then the conversation moved to what we were doing following a group of VBs down the high way. She said, "Why don't we kill them? I've got the AK." She held it up. She liked that gun. Every so often she'd say, "I drove up, smacked that car and started mowing them down! POP POP POP!"

I told her about my history, about losing my family, about starting the Holmesburg Hospital for Broken Minds hoping to rescue some humans. I added the story about how I'd trapped her and she liked that one.

She had a fun attitude about the whole All-Fucked aspect of the modern era. I asked her if there was anyone she cared about and she said her parents would just have made sure she finished med school, they didn't care about anything else. There was a boy she'd half dated in med school but she said that was mainly for sex and companionship. I said that was what most boyfriends were for and she said that it wasn't serious, they both knew they'd break it off when they moved away. Then she added that she didn't really care if he ate squirrels now and ran around naked and I thought that was kind of harsh, but I liked how much she was getting acquainted with the way of things in AFE.

The group we are trailing is jogging south and we are inching along, staying a couple of blocks back, just marking where they are. Meanwhile we are getting into denser and denser houses. We are so focused on them, we don't think about being a slow moving vehicle, and then there is a smack against the window and we're surrounded by hammering. A pack is trying to get into the vehicle. She starts driving fast. I tell her to turn at the next street. I lean out the window and whap them off the car. When we get clear of that pack I realize we can't continue in the vehicle. There are more and more VBs back in the city and the vehicle makes us too obvious.

I say, "Look, go back to Holmesburg. It's marked on this map. Feed those guys and if you're up for it change their diapers, but you don't have to. This mission, I know it's dumb, but I got to do it. I got to try everything."

She says, "You must have really liked her."

I nod. She says, "Look, you might be doing something stupid, but you saved my life, and you're the only person left, so I think we should stay together."

I say, "We're even on the life saving thing."

She says, "Oh, I'm not about that pay back stuff. Guilt sucks and you're weird. I'm just doing what I want, and now it's following along."

I try to convince her some more but her attitude is really gung ho. We drive along until we catch sight of our group again, then we park the paddy. I'd already suited up with Ackee and a bow and she had a spear I'd made and the AK. I explain to her about the AK. I say, "You shoot that thing, we're going to have to fight a thousand blood-mouths and we don't have that many clips and I can't lift Ackee that many times."

"What do you call that club?"

"Ackee."

"That's a funny name."

"Theresa is a funny name."

"You call me Dusty anyway."

"That's 'cause you're still dirty."

She laughs. It was nice to make fun of people and have them make fun back. It was like civilization had returned. She'd agreed I could call her Dusty. She didn't look like a Theresa to me. More like a Sandra. Or a Dusty.

"Really," she said, "What's Ackee mean?"

Dusty was from the suburbs. I say, "In the hood we used to have these Muslim brothers that would sell fake Nike, Adidas, whatever on the corner. And they called everybody Ackee, so then people started calling fake brand stuff Ackee. Then it came to mean anything that was half-ass or not nice. So I made this and it looks kind of ugly but it works, so that's its name."

117

She looks at it. She says, "I think it's nice for what it does."

We're shadow jogging, but it's mid-morning and the light is kind of hard to stay out of. We meet a few VB packs but with two it's easy to deal with them. We're getting down past Olney, and then even past Kensington where I lived by myself, into Old City, and we reach these old brownstones and we see the pack arrive at their den. There are about twenty VBs in the street, naked, hopping over cars. They nuzzle the returning group, squawk some shit at one another, and go on with their business. The whole street is filled with them, and then they keep going in and out of the houses.

Dusty says, "There are a lot."

I've never seen a nest like this. Normally one hundred is a big pack, but it appears the group I met at the Pink Bedroom House is only one fifth of this pack. She adds, "How are you going to figure out if she's in there?"

"I'll go knock on the door and ask, 'Is Angie here?'"

"Funny."

I guess I made the joke 'cause I didn't really have an answer.

32. Is Angie Here?

The solution to the problem isn't actually that complicated. It's a question of technology and time. I have some of the first, and plenty of the second. Dusty and me climb up through some houses until we find a way onto a roof. There we set up with some binoculars.

She lies out on the roof and the lines of her body, the big rise of her thighs and butt, I see it. I hadn't thought of her as a woman up to that moment, she was a baby or monkey or something. It's hard to be attracted to someone whose diapers you are changing. Of course, she's still in the sweats and big tee-shirt I put her in.

"What are you looking at?" She asks. She's got her neck craned around and catches me taking in her shape.

"A woman." The way I say it kind of shocks me. If that happened with Angie, before we were a thing, she caught me checking out her body, I'd have turned red and went and hid, ostrich style, which was pretty much the only way you could hide in that house. It was that small and we stayed away from the edges.

She said, "You sound like John Wayne."

I said, "John Wayne's got nothing on me."

"Oooh!" We laugh.

But enough wasting time. I get down next to her and point the binoculars at the street with the nest. We watch them come and go. I tell her that Angie has got real dark hair and is short. She was lean too, but they are all lean so that doesn't really enter into it. She says, "How long do you need to watch this place before you give up?"

I don't answer which is my way of saying forever. She gets bored of trying to talk to me and tries to sleep, but the late fall wind is whipping, and it's kind of cold. She says, "Can I go find a bed downstairs to sleep in?"

"No."

I tell her she can go get blankets but she can't sleep out here, in the unprotected, VB filled world, unless she's where I can see her. She goes down and comes up with an armful of blankets. She arranges them and rolls up. Soon she is sleeping. I glance at her and think it's funny how, sleeping, she could be VB or human. There's no way to tell a difference.

I wonder at why so many VBs are gathered in one place. Then I see it. A VB comes out of the house. He's clearly an alpha, because the others are either touching his knees or sort of dropping their heads and mincing away as he walks down the street. The other thing that makes him an alpha is his size. He's like a head taller than the others and his shoulders are massive, bull shoulders, so big his head sort of juts forward rather than up, pushed there by the mass of muscle mounding on his back. Behind him are twelve or thirteen more big ones that run in a line.

Sometimes I've noticed this, the size of the pack being directly proportional to the size of the alpha, but I've never seen an alpha like this. After he leaves the house, jogging west, a lot more come out of the house, like one hundred at a time. They're screaming and banding, trying to put together groups to go on the day's hunt. I'm trying to look at all of them, but it's too much and soon bunches of them are heading off, and sometimes I think I see the one I'm looking for, but then it's not, and finally I settle down because the street is pretty much empty.

Maybe I nod off too. She threw some blankets on me. I woke up to shrieking and like normal when I hear that noise I grab Ackee, but I looked around and nobody was up there but Dusty, who was eating some oatmeal like it was the best meal ever and sitting on the bearing wall that separates different house roofs.

"Good morning, sunshine," she says.

"What are they shrieking about?"

"It's a party."

I crawl back to the edge and peer down. The VBs are returning. They come back in the teams they left with, carrying in their hands, and in some cases their mouths, dead things. Rats. Pigeons. Raccoons, opossums. Even a human, a boy who looks eleven years old. For a second I think about what his life was like, how he, like me must have had a family that he lost a long time ago. How he has hid, in cold dark places, lived on Styrofoam Cheetos for months, maybe years. The death might have been the best thing that had happened to him in a long time.

"Fuck," Dusty whispers. Some things med school language doesn't give you the tools to talk about. I nod.

Then I think the kid is kind of good news. I mean not for him, but if he was out there today someone else is too.

The VBs throw their kills on the street. The last one back is the alpha, his hair is red colored, his bull-shoulders are scratched and scabbed, and over his shoulder is a deer. His cohort hoots around him. I'm looking in shock. He brought down a deer.

Dusty says to me, "What? I thought you said they don't use tools."

"They don't."

"How'd he kill a deer then."

"Teamwork. Too much raw aggression. Look at him."

"He looks like a minotaur."

Then I see her. The alpha moves through the crowd of them. The males drop their heads and back away, but the females come toward him, sniff at his body, rub their faces against his skin. One of them has wavy dark hair and a pale small body. She noses into him, staying close, until he returns the sniff. Then she backs away and I see it, the strong lines, the pointy chin. Then I think the face is too similar to not be her, and then I think it's too not similar to be her. I point her out to Dusty.

She says, "She's little."

"Yeah."

"So what are we going to do, Tee. You have a plan to capture her?"

I say something about shooting them all from the roof. She shakes her head. She says, "You already told me and you were right, I've only got a couple clips for this AK, and we're saving those for emergencies. What we need is an efficient but controlled system for killing. Something where we aren't getting tired, but we're killing them, but where we can stop if it's her."

"Sounds nice."

"We just need to think. If we could get them to come into a yard."

"There are too many. They would overrun us."

"What if we aren't in the yard."

"Where are we going to be?"

"Like this! On a roof. We can drop cinderblocks on them. Not too much work."

"It will be on the front end. You've got to spend all that time hauling block."

"So you're rested when you fight them."

I said, "It could work with ten. Maybe thirty. But I see over two hundred here. They would overflow the yard and climb the stairs and we'd only kill about ten before you were using the AK, and even if you got a kill per bullet we'd still die on the roof."

She doesn't say anything, just sits there thinking, her med school brain working hard. I'm a little annoyed that she thinks she's the one who is going to figure this out. Then there is a stop in the shrieking and we look down. The VBs are eating the flesh and not a sound comes from, except an occasional loud pop when they tear a thick piece of cartilage.

I say, "Look. This is what we have to do, hunt each group when they leave. The two of us can take ten at a time, and eventually we get the number down, and then we kill the group.

She shakes her head, like this is stupid.

"Who made you the boss," I say. "I've been living here figuring this shit out for years while you were eating rats."

She just keeps thinking.

"Don't ignore me, bitch."

She looks up at that, and slowly swings the AK until it is pointed at my belly. "What'd you say?"

"Chill," I say.

"Did you just call me bitch?"

"You shoot that, that whole pack down there is going to get you right after you get me."

She smiles. "Good point. So, we're in this together. We decide together. Your plan is too much work. We can do better."

I think about smacking her dirty face. She says, "You know, you could probably find another girl. Just keep trapping them. Eventually one will be as dumb as her and like you."

I roll back and look at the sky. It's turning gray. I say, "It's about family, not a girl."

"That's replaceable, too."

"You didn't have to come. I told you go back to Holmesburg."

She says, "Okay. Just checking how motivated you are. With my genius plan we can do it, but it's going to be a lot of work."

"Genius, my ass."

"I'm glad you appreciate it." She practically flounces, flashing a smile at me and the VBs that mill about below.

33. Blow that Shit UP!

I am crouched behind a car. Turns out Dusty's plan was pretty good. The first part is tricky though.

I run out around the corner onto VB block. Almost as one, two hundred VBs look at me. "Hi," I say. I unleash an arrow and give one of them a neck geyser. "Good morning, blood-mouths!" They shriek as one, and then I'm running. I head down the block and around the corner. I run into a door, they are behind me. I run up the stairs. I run to the third floor. The house grunts bearing the weight of them as they fill the house, storming after me. When I get to the third floor I step through a hole that has been sledgehammered out into the next house. I pause and shoot the first one with an arrow, and then run down the stairs. I wait on the second floor but they don't stop and eat him. They are right after me. So I shoot another one and keep moving. First floor. Keep going. I run all the way down to the basement.

Surprise! Another sledgehammered hole into the house next down the row. I step through this and then I'm going back up. I'm on the first floor. They're too close to string an arrow, their fingers catching my heels, so I get up to my fastest speed and keep going. Second floor. Step high, don't let them get the heel. Third floor. This house has a staircase onto the roof, so I'm jumping up three stairs at a time, them behind me running on all fours. As I'm diving through the door it's slamming closed, the air of it brushes my face as I clear it. The door doesn't close and latch. It runs into about seven arms and three heads. Dusty is shoving at it, her back against it and her two feet pushing against the floor. The door bucks back, almost open enough for them to get out. I add my weight, pushing against the door. We start to move it toward closed, with me swinging Ackee at the body parts blocking it open. Great. Then WHAM something big hits it from the inside and the door surges toward us. We're losing this one.

I look over at Dusty. She shakes her head. "Plan B," she says. We throw open the door and the VBs pile onto the roof. We slam the door shut before another can get in the space and it clicks locked. In that opening moment though, a big pile of them got through. Dusty is running for the AK, and I'm right behind her. Behind me are snarls and infected teeth. Right behind me.

She shoulders the weapon as I dive. TAC. One drops. TAC. Another. She has adjusted the weapon to semi-auto. I grab the rope and pull. SLAM! I hear the front door close. We've got them all tucked away in our three house prison. Or at least most of them. There are some up on the roof with us. I grab my bow to help Dusty. TAC goes the AK. Swiizup goes the bow and arrow.

Then I see him, surging across the roof toward us the same as a tidal wave rises toward a beach village. The alpha. They are close behind him, the outliers out front are just little striplings compared to the massive male and his entourage.

"Him," I scream.

She fires and hits his buddy. "You missed," I yell. They are closing. We've run the length of the block and our backs face a three story drop. They are advancing at an unbelievable pace. They are only four roofs from us, and crossing each roof in two leaps.

"No shit." She shouts back. The AK says TAC. Another body falls, his blood stained mouth smashing into the silver coated roof.

"Hit HIM!" The others are big but he's a whole other size. Then she says, "Shit. It's jammed."

Terrible timing. I run at them. Four big guys, the one in the middle like a dinosaur fighting robot in a sci-fi movie with a little guy inside him and I'm running at them? I'm too close to Angie to die though. I dive roll to one side, Ackee swinging, and I catch one of them good enough to make them think I'm the primary threat.

I'm bounding back down the row, and they leap behind me. Every time I turn to check the gap between us, they are in the air leaping just like Santa's reindeer, I mean, not a one has a foot on the air, they just suspend there in the air, and we leap together, like I'm Rudolph and these crazy hungry motherfuckers are Dasher and Blitzen.

Then the moment is gone, and I hear their snarling. We're coming up on the far end of the row and I won't be able to dodge them twice. They're too smart for that.

I stop dead, planting both feet and swing hard. The biggest guy sees it and pulls up. The shot lands in the neck of one of his buddy's. In one motion I wrench upward, opening holes where each tine has landed. Blood bubbles up in the space the metal leaves.

The other three start to circle me. I'm kind of past last thoughts, so I just focus on backing away so I'm not surrounded, but slow enough that I don't come to the edge of the roof too soon. I keep feinting with Ackee but they don't really care. The one I hit back down the other end is loping down to join up. Guess he doesn't need blood to live.

I glance behind me. Clean three story drop into concrete. It's more like four stories with these high-ass downtown houses. So I figure I'm just going to take my biggest swing at the big one. He gave maybe-Angie a nuzzle and that shit pisses me off. I lift up my old bike-shaft-weapon and say a prayer to the god of humans. "Let me kill his ass." I bring it down. I may never have swung it that hard.

Pop. He's holding it in his massive hand. Then he wrenches it out of my grasp and hurls it. It sails off like a rocket ship.

34. TAC TAC TAC

TAC. The most beautiful sound in the world. The bullet rips through one of the buddies. Looks like she got the gun working. TAC. There goes another buddy. The alpha doesn't understand what is happening, and it makes him furious. He grins, or flashes his teeth, great solid white chunks. I will shortly be the stuff between them. He leaps at me and I duck. Not low enough. My face is mashed against his hard stomach. His massive hands grip at my ears, search for my neck. I grab and hold his thighs, anything to stay away from his mouth, where the virus is- even if it's me up against his smelly crotch. She has to shoot now. I don't care if she hits me too.
TAC.

She missed.

No, she got him. A little spurt out of his forehead and the strength is gone from his arms, and he's falling over me. "Get off," I say, squirming out from under the giant carcass.

Dusty runs up. "Yay! Yay! Yay!"

"Calm down," I say.

"What? Did you just see that shot? Right in the head?! I saved your life. "

"Whatever, we got work to do."

She says, "You wish you took that shot."

I say, "I wish we didn't use the gun."

She follows me back to the three houses we've got them locked in. These houses we fixed up perfect. We blew out those walls so I could lead them all in a snake like path through, up and down. That's hard work in this era. We couldn't use sledges. We didn't use hammers. We used nails and stuff, scrapping away the mortar in the joints. That took a couple weeks.

Then we had to block the windows. The first and second story windows we used cinderblock and brick. On the third stories we used plywood. Now we have them trapped up in there, hundreds of them. It won't hold long. There is a fingernail scrapping at every weak joint, a hand pulling on anything they can get a grip on.

We have to get them distracted. "Reload the gun. We might need it again."

That is the other factor. Now that the gunfire has sounded the streets below are filling up with more of them. I hear them shrieking down below.

I go to the middle house. A double sheet of plywood is there. I pull it away. Milling below, pulling up floorboards, is a dense crowd of VBs. They see the light, and then me, and start screaming. I grab up a ten foot staff with a pointy end.

Dusty remarks, "Why couldn't your girlfriend find a pack of like, ten VBs?"

I drive the spear into a medium sized VB. "She likes people," I say.

"You mean she's an extrovert."

The VBs are now jumping and shrieking. I pop another one. The angle is perfect to drive the point over the collar bone down into the heart. You know a heart shot 'cause they just drop when you get it. Otherwise there is a lot of shrieking and grabbing. Sometimes the grabbing is so much I need Dusty's help to yank the spear back.

When I catch my breath I say, "I don't know what extrovert means."

Dusty laughs. "It just means social. There really isn't a need for that word anymore I guess."

"What's the other one? A person who isn't social?"

"Introvert."

"I wasn't social for a while."

She laughs. She has a spear up too now and is stabbing them fast.

I say, "Slow, you might get her."

She says, "I don't care about your zombie-ass girlfriend. I'm just doing this 'cause you're the only person." She does slow down though.

Then they start climbing one another. Grappling for the roof. I stamp on fingers. They don't care much about pain, but a broken finger is a bad climbing tool. I spear one who is up on the others' shoulders, his torso clear of the hole. Then a quick kid is up out of the other side. I tell Dusty to shoot him and keep spearing. TAC. She's got the gun to her shoulder. The kid goes down.

"THE LID!" I yell. Dusty grabs the lid and slides it back across. A body or two in the way, as the boil of anger forces them up, but I stamp down hard and she gets it across. I jump up and down on it, so it smacks them down again and again, while she hammers in some nails. Actually she just bends them. So I get her to jump on the lid while I hammer it in. They bump against it, and we sit on it and hope it doesn't give. They stop. No more bumping, just a faint sound, like someone enthusiastically eating chicken.

She says, "Why are they stopping?"

I say, "They got enough food now."

"Oh," she says. "You know your girlfriend is probably eating too."

I shrug.

She says, "Yeah, not really a surprise she's so weird. After all she went out with you."

I grab the dead kid who climbed out and lug him to the edge of the row roof and over the edge. He topples down to the street. I don't want to encourage them, but I also want them less hungry. We walk over to the next house. She kicks the plywood lid back. There is only one there. A female. Small, but blond. I spear her. Dusty says, "They're at the feast?"

I yell into the hole, "Hey, blood mouths. Come on out." Three or four trot up the stairs and we spear them. We wait and scream and eventually more turn up. Then they get slow. They've already eaten.

133

She says, "This could get boring."

Our spears are caked in blood. With each jab we need to pierce the flesh, split the tendons and punch into the heart. If we don't hit hard enough we have to wrench the spear back out, and do it all over again. Each jab is hard work. Our arms are tired. "Lunchtime," I say.

She says, "About time, boss."

She walks over to the place we've set aside, on this long section of roof, as civilization. There is food, two folding chairs. The way her shoulders move, under her sweater, seems strange. They seem so delicate but then when she's handling a spear or an AK it's no joke. I reach out and give her a little backrub.

"You better not have blood on your hands," she says.

"Only a little," I say. Hey, it's the end of the world. Everybody does.

35. Up at Holmesburg

It was a lot of work to turn three old city row houses into a maze slash prison, but we had other work to do too. We had to go up, every other day, and help the inmates back at Holmesburg. We'd hike out using the alleys and rooftops, to ninety five, where we'd locked the paddy wagon. Ninety five has lots of abandoned and crashed cars on it, but in the months after the initial flash infection, people cleared a path and you can move at about thirty an hour on it.

Holmesburg is nice. We got indoor spaces with a little heat from the fire places. We know the doors are locked. We don't have to keep looking over our shoulders, which is great.

The rag diapers get pretty bad after two days. Our second trip back up there, she was changing diapers and she yelled, so it echoed off the vaulted ceilings, "Why do we do this?"

I left the cell I was in and came to her, speaking in a quiet voice. I explained the whole business of saving people by separating the VBs out. I didn't understand it but at least it had worked for her. I added a little lecture about volume in AFE.

"I mean the diapers. Why the fuck do we have to have diapers." She hadn't gotten the point about volume. Her face was screwed up as she tried not to breathe the air. She was changing Ogrish, the largest female I had ever seen, with a lower jaw that was half her face. She had large black shit that smelled like ten rat babies crawled into a ball and died.

I explained how we needed to humanize them. I told her how I read books, kept their diapers clean, and also talked nice every chance I got. She made some remark about how the cuffs, the chain, and the duct tape must really help with that. I didn't answer because she was just talking.

After she finished the diaper and came out in the hall she said, "You did all that for me?"

I said, "I did it for humanity."

She said, "No boy ever changed my diapers and read to me before," and gave me this big hug. She turned and walked into the next cell. She started to take off the diaper, and then she said, "I can't do this."

She left, and I did the rest of the diapers myself.

I found her up in the tower. I sat down. It was cold and she scooted up to me and we sat thigh to thigh. She said, "I decided to have two today." She was drinking whiskey. I could hear a slur on her words. I decided to drink none. One of us would need to be ready. "Don't make that face," she said. "You're so judgy."

We sat there for a while, and she said, "Look. I don't think your civilizing them out of infection is working. I think it's probably that they interchange updated forms of the mutated virus and that keeps them sick, but if you separate them out, their body eventually overcomes it."

I said, "What?"

She said, "I'll explain."

I said, "Don't. Listen. My shit works. That's all I know. If you have a different thing we should do, and a good reason, let me know, but this works so we're doing it."

She said, "Fine. Don't listen to me, I'm only a doctor."

"Med student."

I made her come downstairs and we read *Harry Potter* to the crazies for a little.

The third time we went back up Foxy came out of it. He looked different than Dusty had, mostly scared where as she had looked wild. Dusty tried to talk him down, but he retreated the length of his chain and curled up in a ball. He fluttered his eyelashes, like the wings of a baby bird fallen from the nest, half wanting to watch us and half wanting to close his eyes so it would go away.

I waved her off and went in there. "Hey, Foxy. We're leaving the cuffs on, and we're taking off the tape. You can talk and eat then. Also you can change your own diapers. If you scream, that crazy bitch right there will kill you and I'm not going to stop her. I'm not that sane myself."

137

She looked at him kind of fierce and she did look disturbing. She was still a little dirty, and she had the AK strapped to her back. She had assorted knives tucked into her belt.

I ripped Foxy's duct tape off and Dusty gave him some canned food. He thought for a second about eating it and then decided he was too hungry to not eat. One can of baked beans, one can of collard greens, and a tin of sardines and he was still hungry. He hadn't talked yet though.

Dusty said, "Maybe he's still VB."

"VB don't eat collard greens."

I gave him the tour, showed him the VBs in the cells down the hall. I remembered how unsuccessfully this had convinced Dusty that I was a good guy. He couldn't tell they were VB; he didn't know what that was. All he knew was I had imprisoned and duct-taped a lot of people. So I took him to the tower and pointed out how bad the neighborhood was.

When he finally talked he said, "How's Mike?"

Dusty said, "Probably dead, but if not, he's out there eating rat flesh, but he'd rather eat you."

Foxy looked at me for confirmation and I nodded. He looked bewildered, and then he sort of settled into it, like it all added up and it wasn't much more than zero. After that he put his pretty head on his arms and started crying.

Dusty said, "You must have really liked Mike."

I motioned for her to shut the fuck up. She looked at me like why was I babying him. After he cried for a little I patted his shoulder. When he looked up he asked if there was a shower. "I smell terrible." Dusty started laughing.

I told him there wasn't a shower, there wasn't a toilet, and there wasn't electricity, but at least we were alive. We got him into a bed, just leaving the cuffs on one hand, chaining him to the frame. I told him he couldn't run but if he didn't believe us I would give him a tour of the outside world in the morning.

He said, "I don't want to go out there."

He went to sleep, slumped out under the blanket like he was going to try to sleep through the era. He did manage to sleep over twelve hours.

Dusty said, "I wish it was Ogrish. She'd make a fighter, and we wouldn't have to change her diapers. Foxy's weren't that bad."

I said, "We need everyone."

The next day I showed Foxy where the tee-shirts were, how to pin them around the legs to make a diaper, and how to change the used ones. He was good at it, gentle, and careful, unlike Dusty who sometimes punched resistors in the balls. When we finished with that I asked him if he would read them *Harry Potter*. He made a face.

"Do you have *Fifty Shades of Gray*," he asked.

Dusty laughed. I looked around wondering what that was and Dusty explained it was a book that was like romance porn. Dusty took him to the book room and he came back with *Twilight*. "You guys are going to love this." He sat down and started reading but Dusty left. I listened 'cause it was new, and at first I liked the main girl, but once she met the vampire boy it got really stupid really fast, with her saying his eyes caused electric shocks in her body. I left.

After a day I told Foxy we needed to leave, that we had an important mission, but that he should stay there and keep doing what he was doing. I was real insistent about him not leaving but that kind of surprised him. He said, "I'm not going out there!"

After that we didn't go back up as often, maybe twice a week. Foxy was real good at his job, and he was always super excited to see us. When we were there, three people, all different, it was possible to imagine the world being saved, us setting up a little farm or some such shit and making it go.

Dusty would get mad when we left. She was like, "I can't believe we're risking everything for some chick. This is the future of humanity."

I repeated how she didn't have to go. She'd say that she was going to try and help me and keep me alive if only because she wasn't sure she could make it alone. She just said that the whole mission seemed unnecessary and I just told her she'd probably never really been loved, which she said was probably true, and how come someone little and ugly like me had been loved.

There wasn't really answer so that one kind of hung there.

36. Angie?

After lunch it's back to the grind. I set my foot against the lid and slide it back. The VBs in our row home jail aren't leaping up anymore. They barely glance up when we pull back the lid and let the sunlight in. They lie on the ground, or on top of one another, their bellies round lumps on their skinny frames. I spear the ones I can reach from the hole. Dusty spears too.

She says, "You ever worry about the ethics. I mean if they could come out of this and be people again, aren't we murdering them?"

I says, "I thought of that. Then I remembered this is the end of the world."

She doesn't say anything but I can hear her mental gears turning. The point I'm making is this: right and wrong don't matter when survival is that hard. That shit is for people in some nice world. Living is good, dying is bad. That's the whole deal.

She says, "Yeah, but you feel all bad because you hid in the basement instead of dying with your friends."

I say, "That's different. I don't owe these people anything."

She says, "So it's all about debt? Is that how this works?"

I can't explain it to her. I notch an arrow and neck shot one that is lying by the stairwell, too lazy to come up. We watch as the wound turns red and then becomes a stream.

She says, "I mean, you got to do what you got to do. But it's wrong. The only one who is keeping this account of your bad shit is you. All you need to do is move on. You survived. Life is good. Death is bad."

I say, "Hey. Yell something about their mommas. If no more come we're going in."

"In?"

"Yeah, look at them. They're slower than snails."

She puts both of her hands around her mouth to make sure the noise is directed. "Your momma ate my balls." None stir.

"That's disgusting."

She smiles like it's something she learned from me. We drop a ladder in. We get out short range weapons, me with Ackee, her with a knife that is about two feet long. I guess it's really a sword. She wants to use the AK but I don't want any more gunshots. The crowd is big enough as it is.

When the full-ass VBs see us in the house, they try to get out of their piles, up onto their feet, but we get in there quick, slamming their brains into mush. They reach out and we stamp their fingers. They didn't have the foresight to restrain their hunger, and the few who didn't get to eat are the smallest, weakest and slowest. We are covered in blood. It seeps all over; a mud between the fingers, a speckling. There is no shit-talk. It's like how I imagine farmers did their shit when they had to kill cows. Line them up and get on with it.

In the basement in the second house there is a group of them. They haven't eaten and they are up quick and I call, "Retreat." We get back up the stairs so they got to come through the door one at a time, while facing the two of us. I shoot the first one up the stairs with an arrow. The others don't stop and eat him, shouldering past him. They know we're the threat. Dusty is standing to the side and brings her spear up so the tip pierces the next blood-mouth's throat and then drives it in there. I get the second one with a skull puncture, and Dusty is coiled for the third when I see a small frame and dark, almost black hair.

"Hold it," I say. I grab her arm just in case. The small girl breaks out the door. I slip a lasso over her head and yank. It cinches and she goes down, clutching at the rope. Then she starts shrieking.

"Get the rest," I yell.

Dusty is like, "There's ten."

"Stop the door."

"You're so crazy I want to kill you," she says, but she fights back the two that are emerging from the basement, their teeth gnashing. She drives boot stomps into them, forcing them back through the door. After every stomp she sends out a knife jab. She slams and bolts the door.

She walks over and kicks the little girl in the ribs. The blow knocks all the air out of the dark haired girl.

I say, "Why'd you do that?"

"To shut her up."

I say, "That was out of hand."

"Whatever. I'm stressed." I got duct tape gagging the girl and cuffs. We dragged her up. When we get outside up top it's late afternoon, still light, but it's not going to stay that way. I look at the dark haired girl, and then I'm sure. I say, "Hey, Angie. Hey, baby."

She leans her head toward my shoulder trying to bite me, but she's got duct tape over her mouth, so it's mostly just nuzzling, with intent to kill.

Dusty says, "Isn't that sweet. Your girlfriend wants to eat you." There is a pause and she says, "Don't get any weird ideas, TC."

I need a minute and walk across the roof. I look at the skyscrapers, mostly still standing. The tears come and I just let them. It feels like there are a lot of them about to come, but two dry hot ones squeeze out and then it stops. I go back and pull out some clothes I packed if we got her. It's weird 'cause I want to be gentle with her, but she's violent, jerking and jumping. I pin her with my knee and drag on a pair of sweats. Then, I crush an arm with my hip while Dusty holds her body, and get a t-shirt on.

"Nice girlfriend."

I ignore Dusty 'cause there is nothing to say.

She says, "We don't have to do this."

I say, "It's done."

145

She says, "No. You don't owe her anything. This guilt thing of yours makes me so mad. What are you paying for?"

I look at Angie who was rooching around on the ground like a click beetle. I say, "It's not about guilt. It's about wanting to be a person that puts some people, at least the people that give a shit about me, first. Before me."

She looks at Angie too, "That's not a person that gives a shit about you."

"Yeah, it is."

Dusty sees I'm not good for anything, the kind of head space I'm in and does the next step by herself. She drops back into the houses and hauls out some corpses, and drops them down onto the street. The crowd down there goes to work on the bodies, and she goes and drops the ladder across the street to get us off that block. We have glued planks onto the rungs, and Dusty dances across to the bridge to the far block of row homes. The hard part is next. We've got Angie tied up, and Dusty has the rope. She secures it to a chimney. I go across, walking Angie in front of me. She could jump. It's entirely possible.

37. Dusty and Me Flashback

We kept making treks back up to Holmesburg while we worked on the three row home maze trap for Angie's pack. One time, the moon came out early and it was pretty full, and the streets were packed with blood mouthed hunters, so I told her we needed to hide. We pulled up at a quiet block in Frankford, and after some reconnaissance went into the houses. It was still cold, and we secured the doors of the houses and hung them with bells, and went up into the second floor. Dusty looked for bedding, making sure we weren't going to sleep with no raccoons. I attached a rope ladder out the window, just in case. Five exits, just like Jim taught me.

She only found one mattress not shredded by raccoons, and it was a single. We probably would have slept together anyway, with how cold it was. The second we were down though, she turned to face me, the places where her body was shaped different touched mine. She pushed her lips into my face. I pulled back.

"What?" she said.

I said, "What are you doing?"

"I like you," she said. "We're the last people."

I got out of the bed. I said, "Yeah. There will probably be more people soon. We already got Foxy."

"I don't like him. I like you."

147

Part of me really liked the idea. Not just 'cause there was attraction, but 'cause I felt lonely, in a kind of permanent way, and it seemed like being with her might wash that away. But another part of me felt like it would be a betrayal to Angie. Angie was the only girl I was ever with, and even if I wasn't the only guy she was ever with, and I didn't know if she was alive or dead, I didn't want to cheat on her.

And I was lonely not because of being with people or not being with people, but because I had looked at myself in a soul mirror long enough to know some dark ass true ass shit about myself. Getting down there with Dusty wasn't going to change that. It would make me forget it, for a second, but it would come back a lot harder later. Like I felt like I had to be a monk. Once you get soul mirror vision, you don't lose it.

I said, "I'm sleeping on the floor. We're going to get plenty of people soon, up at the prison. You probably won't like me once a full size dude comes around."

She murmured, "I can't believe you're being loyal to a VB."

I didn't say anything. Outside that big ass moon was sucking at the world, pulling oceans toward it, and people's hearts too surged up in their ribcages, trying to find something that big, clear, and clean to guide them, and the hungry things shrieked at it, angry at its light.

38. For the Love

I figure if we make it across the bridge, we're free. The block of row homes we're on is surrounded by agitated VBs, but the next block is far enough away, and off its roof we have a walking exit, and then we're only three blocks from ninety five and the paddy wagon. The only thing between us and Holmesburg is this rickety plank bridge across the street below.

I hold Angie from behind. She has a little jump every couple steps but I got both hands on her, and Dusty is keeping the rope taut, pulling her forward. Angie doesn't feel strong, more like a little bird that falls out of the nest, heart beating between bones made of air and cardboard. She's so wild the touch of something civilized might destroy her, like if you pick up a baby bird its mom will never come to it. Then she really starts to struggle. She leans forward, and then pushed back against me. And lurches for the side and I barely hold her from going off the plank bridge. Then she gets calm. We're going to make it.

No. She lurches violently to the right; I throw my weight the other way. She stops out there, leaning one way with me going the other, a human triangle, and then she comes back toward me, hard. I catch her and we topple together, spinning.

We hit the ladder bridge with her face and my ear, and spin off it. We free fall until we hit the length of the rope. It catches us, and we swing in an arch that starts down toward the street and then curves sideways toward the

149

brick wall. Even before we hit we have big problems. Her duct tape ripped off as we slid off the bridge and her shriek rends the air.

WHAM. We slam against the wall, her first and me sandwiching her up against it. Her air is gone and the long scream is cut off. I look up.

Dusty is straining against the rope, but can't hold it anymore and we drop. We fall a short distance and the rope catches us again. We're only ten feet from the ground, hanging like Christmas tree ornaments. Good thing we secured the rope to the chimney.

"Pull us up," I say.

Dusty strains. We don't move. "I can't," she says.

I'm thinking we can maybe make it to a backdoor. Angie starts screaming again. I wrap a bunch of duct tape around her face. Answering shrieks are coming from out front of the block, where we fed the corpse-eaters.

I check for Ackee.

Dusty says, "You got to cut her off."

I shake my head.

She says, "They won't hurt her. She's one of them."

I say, "You get her back to Holmesburg. You hold her until she comes through. And tell her about me. Tell her I'm sorry."

Dusty says, "I don't care about her, TC."

They're rounding the corner. Sprinting, must be at least thirty. More, they keep coming.

I say, "I saved your life. Do this, we're even. Promise me."

Dusty nods. Angie looks at me, wild eyes.

"Thank you both," I say. Then I let go. I fall the ten feet, landing on my toes and slip Ackee off my shoulders.

They come ten abreast, and they're pouring from both ends of the block. "Come on, blood mouths. You know I'm getting at least three of your bony asses."

39. Eternal

I'm the best human in the fucking history of the world at channeling the raw surges of adrenaline that the fear of death brings into ass-kicking. It is a tool, something that comes to me when I need it. And looking at these blood mouths I need it.

I hit the ground running, and managed to get them all behind me with a couple nice turns. On one of the turns one of them nicked me, with a nail or something. I wasn't worried about it.

We then took off on a race down Fourth Street. We passed by houses that had once been beautiful, three stories, with carpentry that had been preserved with so many coats of paint, carpentry that went back to when Benjamin Franklin was walking the block. I mean, it was preserved up to the moment that the world blew up. I spot an open door. I go through it, slamming it behind me just as I clear. The door bashes the first one in the head and comes crashing back. I hack down with Ackee, two three chops in a row, each one a brutal perfect, and I'm wearing gray matter and red blood, the spatter of war.

"COME ON, BLOOD LIPS. Didn't they ever tell you that I'm eternal?" They keep coming and I keep killing and as much as they are wild, I am wild. But like I say, my wild is controlled. I take the raw instinct of fear and turn it to survival, more than that- to ass-kicking. None of them get through, piling up there at the door. Then I feel shooting, great pain in my calf and I look down. A head, eyes rolled back toward me, teeth embedded in me, is there. Stuck to my leg. Even before I think that it hurts, I think, "VIRUS."

"AGGH!" With a downward jab, two hands on the handle, I get the tines of Ackee in the head, and wrench sideways so the head breaks open like the pieces of a coconut. It's too late. There on my leg are the ten, twelve wounds, in two algebra shaped arches where the teeth broke my skin. It's inevitable. Then I remember Jim's cries as he fought his last fight.

Some of them must have went around back and came up through the basement. Ten maybe. I should have seen it.

It makes me sad because I thought I might get to talk to Angie when she was Angie again, but then too, I always thought I deserved this, and even if I hate the virus it's okay. This is the thing I wanted too; I wanted to save her, and I did. If I cry while I fight, it's because this life was fat full of good shit. I don't want to leave it.

I kill them all without thinking about them, Ackee as fast as ever, but I am silent, I don't talk anymore trash 'cause I am bit. They have won even if I kill these ones.

Afterward I climb onto a roof and lie there, waiting for the sleep to take me. Barely a sliver of moon, the night is lit by stars, and the clouds are patches of blackness against the silver pock-marked skies. Suicide never enters my mind, though before I'd told myself that's what I'd do if I ever got bit. Now I'm too tired. I think for a moment about what it felt like when Angie cuddled with me, her head fitting into the crook of my chest and shoulder. Her burrowing her nose against me, me knowing that she

153

loved me. I think how good it was to eat a can of refried beans in a sealed row home with family.

I fall asleep quickly, as high as the adrenaline takes you it drops you just as low, not to mention that a virus is infecting me.

When I wake I stand up. A pink crease slashes across the horizon, the dawn yellow washing away the dark. I feel no urge to shriek, or lose my clothes, and I think that probably with the virus you don't hate clothes as much as come to see them as unnecessary. I walk down stairs and outside, leaving Ackee on the roof. After all I'll be using my teeth and fingernails now. I walk in the middle of the street now, part of the majority. No more hiding in the shadows, tripping along the roofs.

Three naked persons, my people, are coming toward me. I try a shriek but it kind of catches in my throat. One of them responds, and then they start running at me. Am I going to get a hug? Are they overjoyed to see me? Then one of them is leaping at me, jaws flashing. By instinct I duck to the side, leaving in a knee that the leaper hits. He collapses, and I fall on him, punching him hard in the back of the neck. The other two are on me; a female buries her teeth in my shoulder. I have a knife, which I grind into her ear. The other is trying to latch onto my hip, but I keep fending him off. When the girl releases her bite , I turn on him, grab him by the teeth, and swing his body across my back and pull down, so he goes twisting up over me, but I'm still holding the teeth; his neck cracks.

I am amazed. I check the bite on my calf. The teeth broke skin, and tore up my skin. The wound is scabbed with three streams of pus running out. That should have

154

infected me. I got another bite on the shoulder, lucky her teeth were small.

I walk down the road, still in the middle. I kill them as they come, using whatever. My hands are red brown. Ten at a time, bare hands to bare hands. And as much as I said I was the best at riding the adrenaline, it's gone now. I'm calm as a frozen river. I am immune to their bite. I walk into the night, walk into their nests. Most of them don't even wake up. The next day I reek of death, blood caked on me. Flies escort me.

For the first time, VBs run from me. I walk, they run, they turn to the shadows, their shrieks reduced to mice squeaks, warnings, shrilly made mid scurry.

Snow is falling, white flakes settling on me, and everything gets quiet and slow like it already was in my head. I'm like that. Not hot, but unstoppable, falling quiet, calm, a cleansing force.

A little kid comes out of a building. I lift the red streaked two by four I picked up somewhere and he keeps trotting toward me. Must be six years old. His cheeks somehow still got some fat to them, otherwise he's a rail.

"Hi," he says. There is a lot in the word hi. It says, "Hey, I see you there. You are a person, I'm a person. We should say some things." But the main thing it says is "I see you." It's the opposite of being alone.

"Hi," I say.

He says, "Are you blood mouth?"

155

"No," I say. It's like coming out of a trance. He says, "You got bites."

"I know. I'm immune."

"Wow." He just looks up at me. A pack of six are jogging toward us through the snow. They see me, look twice and turn and head for a gap between the houses. "Can I come with you?"

"You don't know where I'm going."

"Where are you going?"

I look down at him, surprised to hear the childish curiosity that is mixed in with the life or death calculation of odds. It's a math I know. It takes me a while to answer his question, because I hadn't thought about going anywhere. I tell him, "We're going home."

His name is Terrence. He has survived mostly in basements and sewers. He is not afraid anymore, just sad, he tells me. He says that sometimes he wants them to catch him. He says he watches the road for people but the only people he saw were running, and they didn't get far. He hasn't seen people for a long time. He didn't know if I was a person. I had clothes and the two by four but I walked like I had no brain, like them, and I was covered in blood. "I'm okay," I say. "I'll take you to a safe place with some other people."

Talking with him reminds me of other people, of Dusty and Foxy. I think how excited they'll be to see this small person. We walk through the long streets toward Pennypack. He offers me Styrofoam Cheetos and I eat them greedily. He asks if maybe can he wet a rag in the snow, and wipe some blood off me? It seems like a good idea.

We reach the massive wall of Holmesburg and I bang against the door. No-one comes. Then I yell. A guy I don't know, massive shoulders, leans out from the tower. "Quiet," he hisses. "Who are you?"

I say, "Tell Dusty Tee is home."

He squints at me. "We don't have a Dusty."

This pauses me until I remember that Dusty isn't her name. "Whatever her name is. Your leader. And tell her I'm pissed she's not Dusty anymore."

He looks at me like I'm crazy but goes in. Terrence says, "If this is your home, how come no-one knows you?"

I say, "It's complicated."

A minute later Dusty pops her head out the tower window. "Tee! What are you doing out there? Rome, go open the door. That's Tee!" I hear a grumble and then the ground level door opens and Dusty runs out and gives me a big hug. She sees Terrence and starts asking him a lot of questions.

"You're bit." The big guy, Rome holds out a spear to stop me entering the prison. "Theresa, he's bit."

She sees it, the two of bites still oozing. "I'm immune," I say.

She shakes her head.

I say, "I got bit right after we separated. Two days ago. I should be changed already."

She says, "You mind if I put cuffs on you, just for a day or two?"

I say, "This is my castle!"

"This is what you built, yeah," she says. "Let's not mess it up."

I shrug, 'cause it's clear Rome isn't going to have it any other way.

He walks up to me, and I realize it's Hairy. "Hairy? This is Hairy?"

Dusty nods. "Yeah, and I'm glad you made it, TC, but we all have names. He's Rome."

"Hairy, I got you off the Boulevard."

They cuff me and we walk in. I see that they've been organizing and clearing trash off the dirt patches. The snow lies even like a blanket on a made bed. Foxy is there and he gives me a hug. He says that he was worried I wouldn't come back and that Dusty told him what I did and he thinks it was really romantic. Then he starts talking about what he's doing for our inmates and how he's gotten four more out of the comma. He goes on to tell me about the plan for the garden. Of course I don't care but I nod anyway. I mean, I'm thinking about Angie.

Dusty comes back and tells Foxy to shut up and takes me inside. It's really warm. I say, "How is it this warm?"

Rome says, "I rigged up a heater. Runs on anything that burns." He points to a little stove running. I say, "The smoke will bring VBs."

He shakes his head. "I got a filter, and I got a diverter so the smoke is spread real thin. I'll show it to you."

"Cool," I say. Everyone else, it's about six or seven people in all, is crowding in the basement room that seems to be the living room. Dusty says, "Everyone, this is Tee, our founder. He trapped you, separated you from your VB pack, when he was the last human. He's why you are human."

They all cheer. It's kind of nice. One of them asks how come I'm in cuffs. Dusty explains about my bites. They nod but don't look too scared. I don't look VB. They have good energy. They want to celebrate, have a feast, and they put some kind of soup in front of me and the kid, but I interrupt all that, when I say, "Where is she?"

Dusty nods, knowing what I want, and leads me away. The others, laughing, happy, start asking Terrence forty questions. "Where did you come from? How are you alive?" We walk down the cell block and a lot of the cells are empty, their iron gates swinging open. I reach the last one and there she is, barefoot, her hair a straggle. She's sitting, looking kind of surprised. I hope, as I see that look that she doesn't bang her head against the bars when she sees me.

I run toward her, and bump against the bars. I say to Dusty, "You have to take off these cuffs."

She says, "That's VB in there."

"Not anymore," I say. Dusty looks in and sees that Angie is up and jumping up and down like a kid who just got what they wanted for her birthday. Happy to see me. Not a VB.

Dusty shrugs and unlocks the cuffs. I clang through the metal gate, and snatch off Angie's duct tape.

"Ouch," she says. Then, "Hi, Teddy-Baby." I grab her with both arms.

40. Epilogue

I could tell you the things we said, the sorries I kept repeating and her telling me it was nothing, and Dusty telling the story of the time I sacrificed myself for all of them, especially Angie, and how Angie said it was better the way it was.

I could tell you how we made Holmesburg into a castle, how we hunted VB and kept them in one wing while we farmed inside and defended the walls. I can tell you how I tried to stay in charge and that it turns out that there are better thinkers than me, and anyway, there is no-one else immune. Also, I'm not that much of people person. So I hunt. The VB kind of avoid me. It's like I'm the monster now. It's the best thing for me. I got used to wandering, hiding, dreaming. Nobody else wants the job.

The thing you need to know is this. As the spring comes, and the first green pops up, Foxy's veggies, and the trees are getting sung to by four million birds, we have hope. We're making something. This thing we're making, it's a little ghetto, and got problems, but it's a new thing. We're growing in numbers. We're trying to get the women pregnant. I focused that effort on Angie. Solely. She says she's two weeks overdue. I say that we'll name a boy Jim, and a girl, Kwanesha.

About the Author

J. Shepard Trott grew up working with his dad on Philly row home roofs and rehabs. His passion for these structures, and the people of Philadelphia prompted this novella. His other published work is a fantasy novel, *Illumen's Children*, and he is currently working on an urban fantasy about teenagers with super powers entitled *The Shining Mantle*.

He is a lucky husband and a proud father of a two-year old. He teaches English at Philadelphia's Central High School, where he also coaches the boys' soccer team.

About the Cover Artist

Back in high school, Adam Smith doodled on his math homework, and loved art class. His work combines his boyhood passions for skateboarding, BMX, and graffiti, and shows his technical training from the Savannah College of Art and Design. He has exhibited solo and in group shows locally and nationally. Currently he is the graphic half of the design company Scouts Honor Media. Follow him through his website, Dear Adam Smith dot com.